CW00419641

Copyright

CONTENTS

THE LADY'S GUIDE TO
MISTLETOE AND MAYHEM

THE LADY'S GUIDE TO MISTLETOE AND MAYHEM

BY EMMANUELLE DE MAUPASSANT

PROLOGUE

Arrington Hall, Buckinghamshire
25th December, 1887

"REALLY EUSTACE, there's no need to cry about it!"

Ursula gave a great sigh. She'd only pointed out that Eustace's wooden guardsman wasn't wearing the proper sort of boots and that his jacket didn't have the correct number of buttons. It was merely an observation. He didn't need to blub! Sometimes, he was as bad as his little sisters.

"Look, he can still marry my Penelope. She won't mind about it. Stand him up and they can say their vows."

With a sniffle, Eustace did as he was told.

"What sort of boots are they meant to be then?" He touched the felt, frowning.

"Leather, of course, extending to the knee. It takes at least five pounds of beeswax to polish them." Ursula was rather proud of knowing such things. "I'll ask Papa if you might come with us next time you're in town and we go to the barracks. It's not far from the Eaton Square house to Hyde Park."

Licking her finger, she wiped a smudge from Penelope's cheek. "I've sat on one of the horses, although I had to be lifted on, since they're all sixteen hands. We might ask for you to take a ride if you like."

A look of terror crossed Eustace's face. "I—I'd rather not. Still a bit scared to be honest, since the pony threw me."

Ursula squeezed Eustace's hand. "Sorry about that. I forgot."

Lots of things about him were rather annoying but he couldn't help it, she supposed. Not everyone could be brave all the time, and she was lucky, after all, being allowed to accompany Papa to all sorts of interesting places.

Her governess, Miss Scratchley, had departed a few months ago and Papa had ended up taking Ursula into the factory for a while. She'd learnt all sorts of things, with Papa showing her how the leather was cut and the machinery which helped shape and sew the various sorts of footwear they produced there.

Next, he'd promised to let her see the order book and show her how to use the various columns to work out what things had cost and what you sold them for. He'd said it would be useful, one day, when she was running a household of her own.

It was all fascinating. Papa was finding her a new governess soon, but she'd much rather go to the factory with him.

Mama—now in Heaven—would be pleased, Ursula was sure, even though Grandfather Arrington disapproved. At their Christmas luncheon, he'd told Papa that he didn't want to hear anything about his "low-class toil" at Fairbury and Berridge, and her uncle had agreed, calling it "vulgar".

It made no sense to Ursula. On a previous visit, she'd heard Aunt Philippa call her mother a "desirable match", because Fairbury and Berridge "did very well", so it seemed rather rum for Grandpapa and Uncle Cedric to make such a fuss.

The business had been in her mother's family for over two hundred years, and Ursula didn't see why earning money from making something so useful should be frowned upon. Moreover, they weren't just any boots! The Queen herself had once shaken Papa's hand, thanking him for supplying the footwear for her royal household, including her beloved Mounted Regiment.

Grown-ups got themselves worked up about the strangest things.

Besides which, there weren't any male Fairburys to carry on with things, her mother having had no brothers or uncles, so what else was to be done? And Papa seemed very good at it.

"Come on, Penelope." She placed a kiss on the doll's fore-head. "Time to wed your guardsman, and then you can ride off on an adventure together."

Extracting two toffees from her pocket, she passed one to Eustace. "Make him stand up straight, now."

Eustace popped his into his mouth and sucked thoughtfully. "I suppose they'll want me to get married, one day. If I do have to, can it be to you, Ursula? I shouldn't mind so much…if it was you."

"But I don't know if I shall." Ursula looked sideways at Eustace. "Get married, that is." She rearranged the lace ruffle at Penelope's neck. "Ladies take husbands so that they'll have someone to look after them, but I'd rather look after myself. Papa says I'll inherit his half of the partnership and I can do anything I like."

"Oh!" Looking altogether dismal, Eustace pulled off the guardsman's hat. "I think I had it the wrong way about. I imagined it might be you looking after me."

Ursula leaned over to kiss her cousin on the cheek. "Don't

worry, Eustace. Whatever happens, we'll always look out for each other."

"You promise?" Eustace looked decidedly uncertain.

"Yes, and we'll never do anything we don't want to."

"Never?"

"Not if I can help it." With a grin, she unwrapped another sweet.

CHAPTER ONE

Castle Dunrannoch
23rd November, 1904

"Wake up, Lachlan!"

Lady Balmore prodded her husband's shoulder.

With a snort, he bolted upright. "What is it, Mary? What's going on?"

"The door!" Lady Balmore whispered. "Someone's there."

"Then answer the damned thing!" Viscount Balmore yanked the covers back over himself, mumbling a few choice words.

"Lachlan!" She shook him again. "I don't think it's Murray or Philpotts. It was such a strange sort of knock—not their usual way at all."

"What are ye talking about, woman! Strange knocking! It's likely the plumbing. Get ye to sleep and leave me to the same."

Lady Balmore returned her head to the pillow but remained alert.

Only the night before, Lachlan's grandmother, the dowager countess, had sworn she'd seen a shrouded figure

7

wafting through her dressing room. It had disappeared before her maid had arrived, of course.

The castle was supposedly brimming with apparitions. There was a headless warrior who stalked the battlements, a wretched chambermaid who ran sobbing through the minstrel's gallery, and the fearsome fetch of Camdyn Dalreagh, first chieftain, who was said to play a ghostly rendition on the bagpipes whenever a member of the clan was due to meet his end.

Lady Balmore had never liked the moor, nor the castle. She wasn't even particularly fond of those living in it. She'd been far happier in their lovely townhouse in Edinburgh. The shops really were most excellent, and there were always friends to call upon. That was where she and Lachlan should be—not here, in the middle of nowhere, having to step into Brodie's shoes.

But what could one do? A frayed strap beneath his saddle was the cause they'd said—and now his brother was no more and Lachlan was obliged to step up.

The old laird had been bedridden these five years and couldn't last much longer. Lachlan would then be Earl of Dunrannoch. She ought to be pleased, she knew, but all she could think of was being obliged to spend the rest of her days in this damp and draughty hulk of granite. It was simply too misery-making!

With a sigh, she closed her eyes. She must make the best of things—and there were only a few more weeks until the Yule season. She'd take Bonnie and arrange a prolonged stay at the apartments in Princes Street, on the pretext of needing to purchase gifts and so on. The younger girls could join her upon completing their Michaelmas term at Miss McBride's Academy for Ladies and they'd have a jolly time of it.

Yes, she'd go up to town. Goodness knows, she deserved some respite from this dreary abode.

She was just drifting off when the knocking came again. Five slow taps, with a lengthy pause between.

Nobody announced themselves like that.

"Lachlan!" Lady Balmore shook him again. "The door!"

"Ah, ye doaty woman! Am I to have nae peace 'till you've had me oot o' this bed?"

The viscount lit the candle at his bedside and shuffled his feet into his slippers. Fumbling for his dressing gown, he continued cursing.

"I'll look noo, then I want to hear nae more aboot it!"

Entering the corridor, all was dark, but for the small circle of light about his person. There were few enough windows, each narrow and embedded deep in the walls. It took a full moon and a cloudless sky to illuminate this part of the castle.

Balmore held the candle aloft. "There's nae a soul here, Mary. 'Tis jus' yer imagination playin' sleekit!"

Shaking his head, he made to return but, just at that moment, the distant wailing began. Balmore froze on the spot!

It couldn't be. Not again!

A full six months had passed since the phantom bagpipes had last been heard; and Brodie's death had followed on the morn. 'Twas Camdyn Dalreagh returned to warn them once more!

With trembling hand, Balmore approached the stairwell balcony, peering into the shadowy depths from which the mournful ululation rose.

It must be Father's time, may the Lord have mercy on him, taking him to his rest.

Balmore sent up a silent prayer.

'Twould be fitting to go to his bedside and hold the old man's hand as he passed to the next world.

His father's chamber was on the floor below. Grasping

the bannister, he felt his way to the cold stone wall and the first downward steps.

All too late did Balmore feel the draught of movement behind him. A great shove in the small of his back propelled him into thin air. Landing on the fifth step, Balmore dashed his skull upon the stone's edge.

As soft footsteps retreated, the bagpipes too faded. The candle which had flown before him guttered, and the darkness was complete.

CHAPTER TWO

Santa Maria Ranch, near San Antonio, Texas
3rd August, 1905

RYE LOOKED up as the door opened. José Luis and Antonio nodded to him as they stepped through, followed by Alejandra.

"It won't be long." She raised red-rimmed eyes to Rye's and seemed to consider saying more but simply touched his arm. "I'll send coffee and some hot water for washing."

Rye had come straight away, not even changing his clothes, the dust still thick on his face. All this time he'd been away, driving the cattle up to the railhead.

He shouldn't have gone. He wouldn't have gone. Not if he'd realized.

Had Alejandra known?

Not that it mattered.

None of it mattered.

"I'm here, Pa."

Rory Dalreagh turned to face his son. But for two high points of colour in his cheeks, he was deathly pale. Rye took the chair by the bed and slipped his hand into his father's.

"I've something to show you, Rye." A folded piece of paper lay on the coverlet. "I should have given it to you when it came but I wasn't ready. Not then. I thought we had more time." He gave the half-smile Rye knew so well, then wheezed and turned away, coughing.

Lifting his father upright, Rye brought his arms about the older man's shoulders. "You have time, Pa." Rye rubbed his back. "Take it slow now."

He saw the spots of blood on the linen, and more on the pillow. Blood in the handkerchief his father held to his mouth.

"Just a bit…short of breath."

His father took the water Rye passed him, managing a sip, though he seemed to have difficulty swallowing.

Rye's chest constricted hard. His father had been getting weaker these past months. Now, his face was etched cruelly with pain and, beneath the thin nightshirt, his body was skin and bone. Rory Dalreagh had always been strong, working on the ranch alongside Pedro, his partner—working harder still since Pedro had died, four years ago.

"Read it." His father's fingers fluttered over the dove-grey notepaper, his voice insistent.

The letter was written in an elegant hand, covering both sides in tight script, and bearing a gold crest.

Dunrannoch Castle
Perthshire
December 18th, 1904

MY DEAR RORY

I hope this finds you well and that you will be kind enough to indulge me in reading all I must impart. Please believe that I remain your devoted step-mother, despite the troubles of the past.

Your father wished to write by his own hand but is indisposed at this time, being beset by arthritis, and by a great depression of spirits, in which we all share.

He has urged me to write to you on his behalf, but please know that I write from my own heart also. I pray that this letter finds you, though it must travel such a distance to do so.

Despite the estrangement that has existed between your father and yourself these thirty years, he has never ceased to regret the angry words exchanged and your hasty departure. His dearest wish is that those offences may be forgiven, and a reconcilement achieved.

I discovered some time ago that you had kept correspondence with Mrs. Middymuckle. Owing to the circumstances under which I write, I was able to persuade that good lady to share with me your address, and to impart what news she felt comfortable to share of your life in the New World.

From her, I learnt of your wife's death soon after your arrival in Texas, following the birth of your son. I hope you will accept my condolences. Perhaps the news I share here may gladden her, even as she watches over you from the celestial sphere, and that what may come to pass shall make some reparation for the injustices of the past.

With sadness, I must tell you that both your brothers, Brodie and Lachlan, have been lost to us within these past twelve months. We need not discuss the details at length, suffice to say that their passing was unexpected—through mishap rather than illness, and that the family has been deeply shocked and saddened. Your father's grief, as you may imagine, has been severe.

Were I to have correctly addressed this letter, I should have named you Balmore, for the viscountcy now falls to you, as your father's heir.

You have built a life for yourself, far from this ancestral seat, but Dunrannoch needs you.

I exhort you to return home, to take the mantle of your title, and to fulfil our best hopes.

With all regard and fondest love

LAVINIA DALREAGH
    Countess Dunrannoch

FROWNING, Rye set the letter aside. He knew the story of why his father had left Scotland—knew that it was the choosing of his bride that had brought the estrangement.

Ailsa had been a companion to Rory's grandmother, Flora Dalreagh—beneath their attention, as far as the earl had been concerned. Even as the third son, Rory had been expected to marry into the gentry. Ailsa had been a rector's daughter. Genteel for sure, but not sufficiently well-positioned to please the Dalreaghs.

It had always angered Rye, this knowledge of how his mother had been treated—and his father, of course.

"They'll have to do without you." Rye spoke brusquely. "They gave up on you all those years ago. Why should you return now, just because it's convenient for them?"

"Duty." Rory lay his head back upon the pillows. "It's the only reason that matters."

"I'll write the reply. I'll explain. What they're asking is too much. Let them find someone else." Rye took up the paper, folded it small and pushed it into his pocket.

"They already need someone else."

Rye placed his hand within his father's. The fingers were wasted thin, the skin papery. He wanted to tell him not to speak this way—that he just needed to rest, that he'd grow strong again.

But that would be a lie.

He'd been able to make himself believe it before he'd left on the cattle drive—but he wasn't a fool.

"It's you they need." His father's gaze remained fixed on Rye's. "I can't make you do anything you don't wish to. A man has to go his own way. I know that better than anyone. But I want you to go, Rye. I want you to be what they need you to be. It's more than a title. There's an estate to run—just like this ranch, but with a lot more people to care for. Your tenants, relying on you to keep things running smoothly."

Rory's face was pale, coated in a sheen of sweat, and his voice rasping but he held firm to Rye's hand. "José Luis and Antonio have witnessed my will, Rye. I'm leaving the ranch to Alejandra and the boys. With Juan coming up for twenty-two and the others close behind, they know what they're doing."

An ache seared Rye's chest. He'd been born on the ranch —had been raised here boy and man. The landscape, the cattle, the horses, the people—they were part of who he was.

And his father wanted him to walk away?

"Pedro's family owned the ranch long before I came in as partner. It's only right that his sons take over.

"Head east, take the train, book yourself a passage from New York. Find your way to Dunrannoch. They'll take care of you. Find you a wife in the bargain, I'll bet! You're coming on for twenty-seven Rye. A man can't stay single forever. Telegram ahead and they'll have her lined right up—some rose-complexioned beauty to make your heart hammer faster than a stampeding herd of longhorns!" Rory's laughter was brief, dissolving in a fit of coughing.

Rye brought the water to his father's lips again.

"I'm just a plain Texas rancher and that's a whole 'nother world. 'Fraid I'll make a sorry excuse for a viscount."

"You're a Dalreagh. We're stubborn and proud but we do our duty." He squeezed Rye's fingers. "You'll do just fine."

He gave his half-smile again. "Besides which, it sounds like it won't be long before the whole caboodle is yours. My father's a tough old goat but you'll soon be stepping into his boots. You'll be more than a viscount; you'll be an earl."

And I don't want any of it, thought Rye. *Only for you to stay with me—for everything to carry on as it always has. You and me on the ranch, Pa. This is all I've known. It's my home.*

Could he do this?

His father's eyes were already closing. He was exhausted from whatever was eating him up inside.

One thing was for sure: Rye was his father's son. If he set his mind to something, he'd do it.

He'd show the Dalreaghs that his father had done a fine job raising him.

"Well, it sounds mighty swell, Pa."

Content to hear the words, Rory passed into fitful sleep.

Rye splashed his face and hands clean, drank the coffee, and reclined alongside his father. With the curtains open, silvered light illuminated the foot of the bed—a bright thread leading into the night.

Rye lay awake, holding his father's hand, listening to the ragged draw of his breath.

At last, the body that had become so frail lay still and calm.

Rory Dalreagh slipped beyond pain, following that moonlit path.

CHAPTER THREE

Arrington House, Eaton Square, Belgravia
Afternoon, 12th December, 1905

TILLY, Ursula's maid, entered her mistress's bedchamber. As had become her recent habit, Ursula was seated at the window with a book, but appearing to concentrate neither on the view nor the text in her lap.

Pushing the door closed behind her, Tilly gave a slight cough and bobbed a curtsey as Ursula looked her way. "His Lordship wishes to see you in the library, miss."

With a sigh, Ursula set aside the novel she'd begun several days ago without reaching further than the twentieth page. It was impossible to keep her mind on anything for more than a few minutes.

Just over three months had passed since her father's funeral. Time was needed—as everyone had been telling her, in the most sympathetic of tones. She wasn't the first to lose the person she loved most. At this very moment, there were probably thousands of young women in London bereaved of their parents and having to face a new sort of future. One simply kept one's chin high and soldiered through.

Such platitudes were supposed to make her feel better. But, of course, they didn't.

On that last morning, she'd kissed her papa goodbye, reminding him that she'd be along around noon to help inspect the new shipment of leather. Though he'd remained reluctant to allow Ursula to spend full days at the factory, he'd begun to take more seriously her desire to learn about the business. Little by little, she'd persuaded him to share the finer points of how Fairbury and Berridge was run, and to allow her to become involved.

She'd been tying her hat when the messenger had knocked boldly at the front entrance, breathing hard from his caper across Victoria Bridge. She'd pushed him into her carriage and they'd set off through the slug of traffic, Ursula all the while trying to extricate more information from Mr. Berridge's lad.

By the time they'd arrived, it was too late. The doctor was packing up his bag. A quick end, he'd assured her—a single seizure to the heart. A moment of brief pain. Nothing more.

Shaking out her crêpe skirts, Ursula stood. An audience with her uncle, Viscount Arrington, was never pleasurable, but she appreciated the need to be courteous to his requests.

She'd been grateful at the time, when he'd made the necessary arrangements and instructed Ursula to stay with the family in Eaton Square. He'd been adamant that the Pimlico house, purchased for being close to the Battersea workshops, was unsuitable—and most especially for a young lady alone.

The change of surroundings had been welcome, since every room in the home she'd shared with her father brought her to tears.

Now though, she was itching to do something, to go somewhere, to escape this terrible feeling of everything being wrong.

Her days contained a cycle of nothingness in which the

afternoon ride through Hyde Park had become the highlight —crushed between Aunt Phillippa and Lucy, with Amelia, Harriet and Eustace seated opposite.

Other days, there was just Eustace and herself, with Aunt Phillippa as chaperone, which was just plain awkward.

Yesterday, she'd mentioned visiting Fairbury and Berridge, to see how they were managing without her father, but Uncle Cedric had brushed away the idea, suggesting that she accompany her cousins on a shopping trip to Burlington Arcade.

So, she'd written him a note, making clear her wish to return to the Pimlico house and resume her regular habits.

She was suffocating at Arrington House, as if part of her had died alongside her father, and the part that remained was desperate to draw breath.

"Your father indulged you far too freely."

From behind his writing desk, Uncle Cedric fixed Ursula with an imperious eye. "Here you are, not far off your twenty-fifth birthday and you still haven't formalized things with Eustace."

Ursula shifted in her seat and gave an inward sigh. At seventeen, Eustace had proposed that she marry him if she didn't find anyone else she wanted. They only saw each other at family gatherings and she'd hoped, by now, that he'd realized it was just a childish notion. There was nothing of substance behind it. They were fond of one another, but nothing more.

Eustace, at the instigation of his father—she had no doubt —had proposed an engagement three times since she'd turned twenty, and she'd refused a proper answer on each occasion. There was no question of love—nor of him having a broken heart. In the intervening years, each time she'd evaded him, he'd seemed almost relieved.

In fairness, it wasn't just Eustace she wasn't keen on. There wasn't anyone she wanted to settle down with (or settle for)—and there had been plenty of gentlemen from which to choose.

During the season in which Aunt Phillippa had presented her at court, at least three young men had paid calls. Even Mr. Berridge's son had made an earnest offer—with a speech on the wisdom of uniting their two houses, as if they were characters in a Shakespearean play.

She hadn't been interested. They'd all been fops.

If she married Eustace, or anyone else, would they let her pursue anything of her own? Or would they be like Uncle Cedric, proclaiming that a woman's sphere was within the home and that to look outside it for occupation was vulgar?

How could she possibly explore her own interests if she was obliged to obey her husband all the time?

Fairbury and Berridge was part of the world of men. The world of activity and commerce, where you made decisions and things happened. She wasn't ready for her life to be a round of morning calls and musical afternoons punctuated by dinner parties and soirées.

"Wifehood and motherhood!" Uncle Cedric banged his fist on the mahogany tabletop. "Those are the occupations that should matter to you, Ursula. This nonsense about taking over your father's business has got to stop. It would bring utter disrepute on the noble Arrington name."

He went to stand by the fire, then looked at her for some moments—as if weighing up what to say next, since she'd given no reply. Ursula sat straight-backed. Her uncle was entitled to his opinion, and, this being his house, she would sit and listen while he gave forth, but it would change not a whit her own position in the matter.

Smoothing down his moustache, he frowned. "It was bad

enough that your father stooped to becoming involved in such unsavoury business."

Ursula blinked twice.

Unsavoury?

Her uncle hadn't seemed to find the profits of that business so vile last year, when he'd requested funds to repair the roof of Arrington Hall. There had been other instances, too, all logged in her father's ledgers.

Her uncle continued. "Your father's marriage to your mother was one of expediency, having no fortune of his own and no expectation of the title with which I am now endowed. Your mother was base-born, with only her wealth to recommend her."

Ursula sucked in her breath.

How dare he! The vile, snobbish, insulting hypocrite.

But Uncle Cedric wasn't finished. His lip curled in an ugly sneer. "It's unfortunate that this is the stock from which you're drawn, but I've always treated you as one of our own, overlooking the disadvantage of your birth. It is with us that you belong, and your marriage to Eustace shall assure you of a place in society. Whatever others may think in private, they shall not dare utter in your presence, once you are allied to my heir."

Through clenched jaws, Ursula spoke with barely-contained fury. "Grandfather was happy enough to overlook my mother's 'disadvantages' when he agreed to the betrothal, with a handsome dowry attached, while the 'unfortunate' source of my mother's wealth has not deterred you from making use of it." A trembling rage was filling her, now she'd begun.

"Such rudeness!" The viscount's left eye was twitching, while the other bulged in an alarming manner. "It is you, niece, who are failing to observe the proprieties! Were I a lesser man, I would dismiss you from this house immediately. As it is, I bid you to keep to your room until you have an apology to deliver and a more civil tongue in your head."

Ursula also stood, drawing to her full—if modest—height, but without intention of leaving.

She still had plenty to say.

"If my forthrightness offends you, Uncle, then I suggest you look to the cause. As to leaving this house, nothing shall give me greater pleasure." She held her chin high. "I'll apply to Mr. Bombardine's office of law in the morning, for full access to my father's papers, and shall arrange a meeting with Mr. Berridge forthwith. You need nevermore be concerned with the Arrington name being sullied, for I shall refute any claim that we are related!"

"Abominable, ungrateful girl!" The viscount's nostrils flared large. "By all means, visit Bombardine, and he shall tell you not only that my guardianship of you, and of all the assets in your possession, continues until your twenty-fifth birthday, but that the Pimlico house has been sold—"

"Sold?" The heat in Ursula's chest rushed to her head. "You cannot mean—"

"I do." He moved to the window, not even looking at her. "The contents were auctioned off last month, and your personal possessions brought here; placed in storage in the attic of this house."

Ursula grasped the table's edge, suddenly speechless.

He turned towards her again, a malicious glint in his eyes. "Your stake-holding in Fairbury and Berridge has been dissolved."

The last he uttered with marked relish.

Dissolved?

Her throat constricted.

Surely not! It couldn't be true.

"You've sold my father's share in the business?" She struggled to project her voice but he heard her all right.

A slow, triumphant smile spread across her uncle's face. "I

see we understand each other. As your guardian, the decision was mine and Mr. Berridge was most obliging. Not only did he appreciate your reluctance to continue an association with the business, but offered a very fair price to release you from the partnership. Naturally, wishing to fulfil my duties, I accepted on your behalf."

Ursula spluttered, but nothing of coherence emerged.

Her uncle made a study of his fingernails. "Of course, the terms of your father's will only allow you to enjoy the interest of that capital, upon the arrival of your forthcoming birthday."

Glancing upward, he fixed Ursula with a beady stare. "Full entitlement must wait until such time as you marry—or reach the spinsterly age of thirty years." He inclined his head. "All the more reason for you to apologize for your hasty words, and fix a date for your betrothal to Eustace."

"And until my birthday?" The question emerged as a whisper.

"The interest is at my disposal, to allocate as I see fit. Several of the rooms at Arrington Hall require refurbishment, and you can have no objection. The house will pass to Eustace one day." He gave her a tight smile. "You'll receive the benefit at last, and your children will, in turn, inherit."

Though her legs felt entirely numb, she managed to cross the thick pile of the Persian rug and reach the door. She knew his eyes followed her, thinking that he'd won, that her immediate lack of means would keep her under his roof—not just for these coming weeks but beyond—that the thought of setting out into the unknown would daunt her.

Viscount Arrington didn't know her at all.

CHAPTER FOUR

The Highland Caledonian Overnight Sleeper to Fort William
Early morning, 13th December

WITH THE LURCH of the train, Ursula was tossed onto her side and almost thrown from the little cot in her compartment. She'd been awake through most of the past hours, she was sure, but the jolt had certainly woken her.

She wasn't in her own bed—neither in Pimlico nor Eaton Square—and it was uncomfortably chilly. Fortunately, she'd slept in most of her clothes.

Pulling on her cardigan, she swung her stockinged feet to the floor and lifted the blind. Light was barely creeping into the sky, the moon fading against a backdrop of delicate violet-grey, yet the landscape glowed white.

And there were mountains!

The sort that loomed so majestically you had to crane your neck to see their jagged peaks. Their ridges and upper crags were heavily snow-topped, while the lower planes and the moorland beneath were crusted thick with frost.

There was no doubt about it. She was in Scotland—and there was most certainly no going back.

If dawn was near breaking, it wouldn't be long until they reached Fort William.

She fought a sudden wave of nausea.

What had she done?

It had seemed the only option yesterday—to pack a large carpet bag and swear Tilly to utmost confidentiality. Ursula hadn't a great deal of coin but enough for the ticket, and for the hire of some transport at the other end.

The note she'd scrawled for Eustace would stop him worrying. He'd always been a good friend. He'd want her to be happy. He'd understand.

And he'd keep her whereabouts secret. It was only thirteen days until her birthday. Once it came, she'd have enough income of her own to live upon. Modestly, perhaps, but enough. And she'd be her own person, without needing to ask for anything.

As for where she might go until then, Ursula had immediately thought of Daphne. Hardly a month went by without an exchange between them, and she'd often mentioned how much she'd love Ursula to visit.

They'd met at the Ventissori Academy. Ursula had hardly been a star pupil but her father had been adamant that she attend, and she'd wanted to please him. Together, she and Daphne had practised how to daintily swallow an oyster and remove a lobster from its shell, how to tell apart their forks for fruit and fish, and how to fold napkins into elaborate whimsies.

Finding everything such a bore, Ursula had resorted to making the other girls laugh—mimicking Monsieur Ventissori's mincing walk and his Gallic histrionics. Daphne had disapproved but always covered for her and, when their Academy days came to an end, had insisted on them keeping in touch.

Daphne was spending Christmas with her parents, only twelve miles east of Fort William.

Once I get there, I'll simply find a cab for hire, or someone with a cart if need be, thought Ursula. It would be wonderful to see Daphne again.

Why then, did Ursula feel like she wanted to vomit?

Hugging her cardigan closer, she searched about for her footwear.

Breakfast. That was what was needed.

All things were more manageable once you'd eaten. She'd find the dining car and order something comforting.

Her life was in a mess but if she was to sort it out, porridge—hot and sweet—and a steaming pot of tea would be a good place to start.

CONSUMING a generous helping of sausages and grilled tomatoes lifted Ursula's spirits. As did the toasted muffins. And the porridge, served with cream and honey.

Meanwhile, the sun rose, flashing into view between the eastern mountains.

Still, a knot continued to pull tight within her chest.

Ursula sighed, wondering if the waiter might be prevailed upon to supply more tea, but he seemed to have disappeared altogether.

The carriage was surprisingly empty but for herself, an elderly lady and a party of three clergymen at the far end.

Ursula was staring dolefully into her empty cup when a kindly voice carried to her ear.

"I've plenty in my pot if you're still in need of whetting the whistle."

With her chin dipped to peer over her reading spectacles, the owner of the voice was eyeing Ursula.

"And the company would be welcome." She inclined her head towards the seat opposite and, with a grateful smile, Ursula gathered her belongings.

"Urania Abernathy," said the lady, proffering a hand much wrinkled, though steady enough in pouring the tea. She delved into the large handbag at her elbow and plucked out a hip flask, adding a tipple of something dark and potent to the darjeeling.

"One needs extra warming at my age." Miss Abernathy took an appreciative sip, then burrowed again into the bag's depths. Withdrawing a bar of Fry's chocolate cream, she broke off two segments.

She and Ursula sat in companionable silence for a few moments, watching through the windows as the Highland scenery whisked by.

"You're visiting family?" asked Ursula, having sucked away the last of the soft-centred fondant.

"Someone's family, yes—but not my own." Holding up a piece of notepaper, Miss Abernathy squinted at the close-written script. "I'd intended some time with my sister on the Dorset coast, but this arrived a fortnight ago. A recommendation through Lady Forres. Most unusual, and generous remuneration. My little holiday shall wait until the new year."

Ursula smiled politely and drank her tea.

Of course, Miss Abernathy must be a governess. Not just her costume—of plain, worsted wool—but her manner proclaimed it.

There, but for my inheritance, go I. Ursula inwardly shuddered. Children were not her forte. The idea of dedicating her life to making them sit up straight and learn their manners was too horrendous to contemplate.

"The grandson of Earl Dunrannoch." Miss Abernathy folded the letter away and rested her hands in her lap. "I've made a special request for the train to stop at Gorton, on the edge of the moor. I only hope that the carriage is waiting. One can get so cold standing about."

Miss Abernathy's pale blue eyes regarded Ursula. "And

you? Family in the Highlands? I know most of the older seats."

"A friend." Ursula was seized by sudden panic. "And her family live very quietly." She gave a tight smile. "Like hermits. Almost."

Urania Abernathy's eyebrows rose into the quiff of her silver hair.

"How unusual!"

She said nothing more, merely settling back to close her eyes.

The contents of the hip flask must have been rather potent for, the next minute, she was gently snoring.

Ursula returned her gaze to the great outdoors. She'd always wanted to visit the Highlands, and here it was— looking just as windswept as she'd imagined. Mile after mile of emptiness. Nothing but the moorlands and the mountains and the huge, open sky. Where habitation did come into view, it was modest indeed. The cottages, red roofed and white-washed, looked large enough to contain only a single room.

What was Daphne's place called? Kintochlochie? She'd described it many times, bewailing fireplaces that refused to draw—or belched smoke, draughty corridors and windows that rattled with the wind. It had sounded terribly romantic —apart from having to eat haggis, which didn't appeal at all.

Daphne's last letter had mentioned a new beau—the heir to a turkey farming empire, in Norfolk no less. Not a mountain in sight. She'd seemed nothing but excited at the prospect, with no words of remorse at having to leave behind all this wild gloriousness.

Ursula's stomach churned, threatening to bring a reappearance of her breakfast.

Castle Kintochlochie didn't yet have a telephone, but perhaps she should have asked Tilly to arrange a telegram. At least, then, she wouldn't be arriving wholly unannounced.

Turning up on someone's doorstep did seem rather an imposition—and so close to Christmas. She'd acted without thinking it through and, now, here she was, hurtling towards a problem—not to mention the sort of weather that gave one chilblains. If Daphne's family permitted her through the door, what might be in store? Never ending haggis, probably, and men shooting things. She might not be able to go for a walk for fear of being mistaken for some poor creature destined to have its head wall-mounted.

But what could she do? Soon, the train would reach Fort William, and she had nowhere else to go.

Perhaps she should confide in Miss Abernathy and ask her advice. Ancient as she was, she must have seen a great deal of life, and she'd made her way without coming to harm.

She was still asleep however—her head lolling with the motion of the train.

Where was it she was alighting—Gorton?

The train had been passing through open heathland cloaked low in mist. Ursula struggled to recall the map. Rannoch Moor was just south of Glen Coe, wasn't it, and there were several private stations before you reached Fort William.

"Miss Abernathy." Ursula leaned forward. "Time to wake up." She touched her arm. "We're nearly there. You'll need to gather your things."

She noticed then that Miss Abernathy was no longer snoring. In fact, the older woman was altogether quiet.

Moving to the other side of the table, Ursula placed her hand over her companion's.

Quite cold.

"Urania!" Ursula gave Miss Abernathy a gentle shake, then squeaked with shock as the old lady pitched forward.

Pushing her back in the seat, Ursula propped her into the corner.

Miss Abernathy wasn't just asleep.

And she wouldn't be getting off at Gorton.

From the front of the train came the blow of a whistle. They were slowing, the brakes jarring on the track.

Was this the place?

A strange horror washed over Ursula.

The train would stop and Miss Abernathy wouldn't get out. They'd come looking for her and find her, dead.

Natural causes of course, but the guard would need to speak to Ursula. He'd ask her questions, and wouldn't the police need to do that too, once they reached Fort William? They'd want Ursula to tell them about Miss Abernathy. They might ask Ursula for her place of residence. They might contact Uncle Cedric.

Ursula stood up.

At the other end of the dining car, the clergymen remained deeply in conversation.

The waiter was still nowhere to be seen.

Without further thought, Ursula picked up Miss Abernathy's voluminous handbag.

I'm sorry, but I have to.

Darting back to her compartment, Ursula threw her own few possessions into her luggage. She donned her coat and pushed her hat down low on her head, reaching the outer door as the train made its final, juddering halt.

Fingers trembling, she pushed down heavily on the handle and stepped out into the grey swirl of mist. Some way ahead, a shadowy figure looked out from beside the engine and waved. After a moment's hesitation, Ursula waved back, and the whistle blew again.

She stood on the tiny platform, watching the train pulling away, gathering speed, then disappearing. Towards Fort William. Towards Daphne and Kintochlochie.

Away from Ursula.

What had she done?

CHAPTER FIVE

On the edge of Rannoch Moor
A little later in the morning, 13th December

ONLY WHEN HER toes began to throb and the tip of her nose went numb did Ursula realize how cold she was. Her navy-blue coat, in finest quality wool, reached almost to her ankles, but was designed more for fashion than insulation. Her gloves and scarf were similarly inadequate. Her hat did nothing to cover her ears.

The mist wrapped around her—a curling, milky haze through which the sun struggled blearily. Where the platform ended, bracken began but she could see nothing more.

No carriage. No one to meet her.

Or rather, no one to meet Miss Abernathy.

Ursula put down the bags and pursed her lips. It was really too bad. A woman of such advanced years could hardly be expected to wait indefinitely in such a remote and exposed location. Ursula felt most indignant on her behalf—not to mention her own.

Someone was supposed to be coming to collect Miss Abernathy, but that someone was late.

Ursula felt a sudden pang at what she'd done—leaving Miss Abernathy on the train like that and taking her belongings. In running away, had she left behind her sense of integrity? Her scruples? She kicked at the rolling mist, which merely shifted about her hem before closing round again.

A still, small voice inside whispered that she'd acted badly.

Walking the length of the platform, Ursula berated herself. A full twenty steps, then she turned and walked back again. It wouldn't matter how far she walked, it wouldn't change anything.

However wicked it was, she had to make the best of the situation.

But I'll do something "good" to make up for my failings. Regardless of how revolting the child is, I'll be kind to them.

At one end, there was a rough cutting through the frosted bracken leaves. Not a road but a track of sorts. Ursula could see no other. From that direction, surely, the carriage would come.

This being the case, oughtn't she to set off? The exercise, at least, would keep her blood on the move. She couldn't just stand here, getting colder and colder.

It couldn't be too far, could it?

And there were hours of daylight ahead, even though the sun was having trouble penetrating.

Where was it she was going?

Ursula knelt over Miss Abernathy's handbag. It was a sturdy thing, though the leather was cracked at the corners and the clasp tarnished. It was a handbag that had served its owner well.

Worrying her lip, Ursula pulled the metal frame wide. Inside, the contents were an unexpected jumble, but the letter was near the top: A pale grey envelope, addressed to Miss U. Abernathy at Kilmarnock Manor.

It was a convenient coincidence: their names being so similar.

Steeling herself to do what she must, Ursula scanned through. She was expected at Castle Dunrannoch on the fourteenth of the month "to undertake lessons in etiquette and manners befitting the future earl—a young man unaccustomed to the circles in which he will be moving".

Apparently, there had been a series of bereavements and the title would be falling to some unsuspecting grandson—a child for whom the family had employed Miss Abernathy.

Except that it wouldn't be Miss Abernathy turning up. It would be Ursula.

And it wasn't the fourteenth of the month; that would be tomorrow.

And, though the mist was as thick as ever, she was pretty certain that it had started to snow.

She gave a strangled gasp of laughter.

How absurd everything was.

Incomprehensibly ridiculous.

If she didn't laugh, she'd sit down on the spot and cry.

Whichever guardian angel was supposed to be looking after her, she assumed they were having a good chuckle as well. Ursula only hoped they might give themselves a stitch from all the jolly good entertainment, because she wasn't sure how much more of this celestial humour she could bear.

Ursula got to her feet and picked up the bags.

Logic would dictate that the track led to the castle, so she simply needed to keep walking until she happened upon civilisation—or whatever passed for it in these parts.

She ignored the quiver in her chest as she left the platform, following the track. A brisk pace was the answer, and her eyes on the path at all times. Never mind that the snow was settling on her eyelashes and her teeth wanted to chatter. The castle might be only a mile or two away.

It was beautiful, in an eerie way—everything white and still and quiet.

And with each step, she was closer to sitting before a fire, being offered crumpets, and fruit cake, and scalding hot tea.

As for the matter of impersonating Miss Abernathy, she was a great believer in the power of charm. She mightn't feel terribly charming at this minute but, once she was warm again, she'd dredge some up.

Onwards she went, the cold breath of the moor on her cheek. The swish of her skirts against the stride of her legs became the rhythmic count to her pacing. She tried to ignore how the bags were making her arms ache.

All had seemed still and silent, but now she heard the invisible. Water trickling nearby. Croaking. A faint hoot.

Then something else.

A distant thud, repetitive and coming closer—though she couldn't tell from which direction. The mist and snow conspired to deaden sound, while her own breathing seemed to grow louder.

Ursula shivered.

"Is anyone there?" Her voice sounded feeble.

She moved to the edge of the track, peering through the pale vapour.

Something was in the mist. There was a snort and a pawing of the ground.

A stag? She'd never seen one but they were huge, weren't they?

With horns.

Ursula was unsure what to do for the best. If she stayed upright, she might be gored through on a candelabra of antlers. If she fell to the ground, she could be ridden under-hoof.

Before she had the chance to decide, the creature was upon her. She saw flaring nostrils and a wild eye, and gums drawn back on huge teeth.

Not a stag but a stallion, its hooves rearing up over her head.

Ursula screamed.

"Whoa there, Charon!"

The man pulled his mount round sharply.

"What the hell?" A deep, drawling voice barked out above her. "I damn near killed you!"

Ursula cowered back from the frisking horse and its irate rider, quite unable to find her voice.

In a single bound, the man leapt down to stand before her.

"What in the name of all that's holy are you doin', wanderin' round like a wraith? You scared the bejesus out o' me."

Ursula found herself looking at a man taller than any she'd seen before. Tall, wide-shouldered and well-built.

Loose-limbed too.

The way he'd kicked his heels out of the stirrups and thrown his leg over the mount's head to jump down, he moved like an acrobat.

She blinked. "How b-big you are!"

He gave a slow smile.

"I mean t-tall! Very tall!" She was chilled to the bone, her teeth chattering madly, but Ursula felt the tingle of heat rising to her cheeks.

"Six foot, five, ma'am. Corn-fed in the heart of Texas."

He held out his hand. "Name's Rye, and I'm mighty pleased to meet you."

Ursula stared at his hand a moment before shaking it. Really, it was all most peculiar.

Texas? Wasn't that where the cowboys lived? It would explain his attire: the most ludicrous hat, and oddly shaped boots—embroidered and heeled. His coat hung open, despite the frost in the air, revealing a checked shirt and soft trousers. There was a red kerchief, bright and patterned, at his neck, and he was unshaven and sun-darkened, like a bandit.

His hands, strong and firm, went to her shoulders, and it occurred to her that he was probably holding her up. Whether it was the cold or the shock of being near-trampled, she couldn't feel her legs at all. They were utter jelly.

Trembling, she raised her gaze to his. His eyes were quartz grey, short-lashed and heavy-lidded, and staring right back at her.

"Miss Abernathy," she said at last.

"Well, Miss Abernathy, it's colder than a blue norther out here." That drawl again, as if he were caressing her skin with every word. "If you're lost, that makes two of us, what with this damned fog."

Her breath caught, looking at his mouth. It was deliciously masculine.

"With this snow gettin' thicker we'd best lit outta here. There's a bothy roundabouts. The vapours shifted just afore I clapped eyes on you and I'm mighty sure I spied a red roof out yonder."

Without waiting for her response, he picked up the bags and tied one to either side of the rear of the saddle.

"You'll be safe up front, with me behind. I won't let you slip."

Ursula looked at his outstretched hand.

He wanted her to climb on the horse with him?

Was he mad?

She didn't know him.

And he wanted to take her to a bothy—whatever that was —where they would be alone.

He must have seen her hesitation. "You've nothin' to fear, ma'am. Charon's a devil when he's scared but he'll hold steady now. As for me, I was raised to be respectful. I'll have ma arm about your waist but I won't take no liberties, however temptin' that may be." His mouth quirked up in a half-smile.

No sooner had her fingers touched his than she was launched upwards, her toes guided to the stirrup and her bottom plonked in the saddle.

As he settled behind, she was aware of his straddling thighs tucked around hers. With one hand taking the reins, he brought the other around her middle, pulling her into his chest, and gave Charon a gentle kick.

She'd only just met him, but he was just what she needed.

A source of heat!

CHAPTER SIX

Rannoch Moor
Later that morning, 13th December

HE SLITHERED off the horse and, without a by-your-leave, encompassed her waist, lifting her down. She stood in the snow, shivering, watching him untie her bags before leading the horse into a lean-to at one end of the cottage.

Resting his forehead briefly to the stallion's nose, he murmured a last endearment before shutting the half-doors.

The bothy itself was damp and earthy, the floor being no more than compacted soil. The single room contained a truckle bed, a table and chair, a cast iron woodburner, and some shelves—mostly empty. It was hardly warmer inside than it had been out, but there was a stack of fuel at any rate —not coal but peat, sliced in thick, dark bricks and stacked dry in the corner. Someone had left a tinderbox and a few sticks of kindling.

Rye bent to the task, placing the wood in a pyramid and coaxing a flame before resting a block of peat on either side.

"Come on, closer." While she unpinned her hat, he drew

up the chair for her, right by the fire, then stripped the blanket off the bed. "This'll be better than your damp coat."

Nodding, Ursula fumbled with the buttons, laying it over the table.

She stood in her travelling skirt, shirtwaist and long cardigan, letting him place the blanket round her shoulders, all the while trying not to think about who might last have used it.

Did the cold kill fleas?

She hoped so.

With the flames rising, he pushed-to the iron door, then made an examination of the room. There were no more blankets and nothing at all to eat or drink, though there was a pan to cook with, and two earthenware cups.

"I'll collect some snow." He indicated the old pan. "Don't s'pose you've a few coffee beans in those bags o' yours?" The side of his mouth curled upwards.

She managed a small smile in return. "There's some Rowland's powder."

"Hot water and tooth powder—sounds delicious." He pulled a face.

While he was gone, she drew the chair closer to the burner and unlaced her boots. Her feet were soaked through. Dare she take off her stockings? She'd more chance of getting them dry if she lay them over something.

She was about to wriggle her second foot free of its worsted when Rye returned.

"Whoa there. I turn my back for a few seconds and you're gettin' bare! Least let me be here while all the excitement's happenin'." He gave her a wink.

"I was just—I really wasn't—" She looked down at her feet: one pale and the other damp in its soggy casing. "I'm being sensible," she said at last, yanking off the other foot of her stockings and tugging down her hem to cover her toes.

"Sure thing." Rye set the pan on the stovetop then

scooped up the cast off underthings. "Like a rattler shedding its skin, huh?" He grinned, draping them over either side of the stove.

Best not to encourage him, Ursula decided. *He's really becoming altogether too familiar.*

In proof of point, having removed his coat and boots, he rolled down his own socks and lay them alongside her things. He gave her a sideways glance and another quirk of his mouth, clearly aware of her watching.

Untying the kerchief at his neck, he used it to wipe his face, but kept on his hat, merely tipping it back a few inches.

He threw another brick of peat into the burner then sat, at last, on the floor, since Ursula was occupying the only chair. One leg he stretched towards the warmth while the other he crooked at the knee, resting his elbow on top.

He was in his shirt sleeves, the fabric tight across his shoulders and arms. His trousers, too, fitted close through the hip and thigh. Where he'd removed the kerchief, the upper two buttons of his shirt were open, revealing tufts of dark hair.

Don't look. He'll only get the wrong idea.

But Ursula couldn't help herself.

She'd seen Eustace's chest only once since he'd come of the age where men grew hair. His, she was sure, couldn't have such a covering. Besides which, Eustace was blond and didn't even have a proper moustache yet.

Rye's stubble looked like it would turn into a beard if he ignored it for a few days.

"A strange place to be, isn't it, on the moor?" She bit her lip. As an opening gambit, it wasn't the friendliest conversation starter. "I mean, are you visiting someone? For the festive season?"

That was better.

"Yup." Rye gave a slow nod. "S'pose you could say that."

"Won't they be worried about you?"

"Maybe, but they told me about this place when I was saddling up. Said I was to shelter here if the weather came in."

He fixed her with his flinted grey eyes. "And what about you, Miss Abernathy? What ya doin' in this neck of the woods?"

She'd been waiting for him to ask. Of course, she had to tell him. Once the visibility improved, she'd need him to show her the way. He must know of the castle, even having been on the moor a short time, and there was nowhere else. She could hardly stay in this bothy.

For a fleeting moment, she wondered if whichever relatives he was staying with would mind having her as a house guest for a few weeks, but she pushed the idea away immediately. Foisting herself on his family would be ridiculous. At least those at the castle were expecting her—or Miss Abernathy, rather. She'd muddle through.

"I'm headed to Castle Dunrannoch," she announced.

"Well now. Ain't that somethin'." Rye's face split in the widest grin.

"I've a post—that is, a position." She supposed there was no harm in telling him. "To teach a little boy at the castle. Table manners—that sort of thing."

"Is that right?" Rye leaned forward. "Don'cha know how old he is?"

"He's just some horror who doesn't know how to behave. It's bound to be awful, but there we are. I'll sort him out."

"I've no doubt you shall, but he mightn't be as bad as you're thinkin'. You might even like the lil fella." His eyes flashed in amusement again.

Really, it was becoming most annoying—as if everything she said was a joke. "Unlikely!" Ursula was reluctant to dwell on what awaited her in her role as Urania Abernathy.

The stove was heating up nicely, the water simmering, making Ursula's mouth water for a cup of tea.

Urania had seemed the sort of woman who might carry a tin of her preferred blend. And there had been the chocolate; Ursula wondered if there were any left.

It seemed rather awful, now, that she'd taken Miss Abernathy's handbag—although she doubted Urania would have minded. Fetching it over, she vowed to send thanks heavenwards if it contained anything edible.

"Y' might have some chicory even?" Rye eyed the bag speculatively. "Water's near boiling."

Ursula popped open the metal clasp and peered in. On top was a ball of wool and a half-knitted bed sock, still attached to the needle. Those, Ursula lifted out and placed to one side. Underneath, everything was a jumble.

There was the flask Urania had produced in the dining car. Screwing off the top, Ursula took a tentative sip. Hot and gingery, it burnt her throat, making her splutter.

"Easy there." Rye was behind her in a flash, rubbing through the blanket as she coughed.

When she'd calmed sufficiently, he dipped one of their cups in the hot water and made her drink.

"What is it?" Ursula wiped at her mouth. Her lips still tingled.

He sniffed, then tipped it back.

"Not as good as the bourbon back home, but pretty damn fine." He made a clucking of approval. "Brandy. And not the cheap sort." He looked at her incredulously. "You forgot this was in there?"

"It's not mine!" Ursula pressed her fingers to her temple. "I mean…it's for emergencies."

"If you say so, lil lady." He gave her another of his winks.

Ignoring the provocation, she returned to the task and alighted on a bottle—too small for alcohol, though the contents were dark. Tentatively, she held it to the light.

"Syrup of figs." Rye squinted, reading the label. "Isn't that good for—"

Ursula shoved it back again. "My last charge. A spoonful every morning." She returned to rummaging. There was bound to be something useful.

Her fingers found something metallic. A small tin! Opening it, Ursula smiled. She'd been right. Definitely tea. She gave it a sniff. An unusual blend—rather smoky. Lapsang Souchong?

She held it out to him. "It's an acquired taste. Very relaxing in the evening."

Rye lowered his nose and sniffed cautiously. "But it's—" He rubbed a pinch between his fingers, looking bemused.

Before she could stop him, he'd reached into the bag himself and drawn out something made of wood. It had a long stem with a bulb at the end.

"You smoke a pipe?" He raised an eyebrow.

Glaring, Ursula snatched it away. "A lady's handbag is sacrosanct," she retorted. "It's not for—invasion."

God help her! She'd be struck down at this rate.

In fact, Ursula hated the acrid smell of tobacco smoke but why shouldn't Miss Abernathy indulge. "We all have our vices." She smiled tightly, trying not to show her disappointment over the elusive tea.

The bag contained many of the usual things—safety pins and a sewing kit, a newly laundered handkerchief, a pocket watch, Epsom salts, a jar of balsam.

With satisfaction, she located the rest of Miss Abernathy's chocolate and three toffees in their wrappers.

"Not bad." Rye gave her his lazy grin again. "But no coffee, huh?"

"It's not the sort of thing women tend to carry about…" Ursula sighed. She really would have loved a cup of tea. Would the toffees dissolve?

The very bottom of the bag was sticky with the remnants of confectionary long-since sucked, but there were the unmistakable edges of a book. Bound in dark blue leather, it was pocket-sized, the title embossed in gold:

The Lady's Guide to All Things Useful

Ursula leafed through the first few pages, her brow furrowing. She'd received something similar from her grandmother on her eighteenth birthday, just before she was enrolled with Monsieur Ventissori and was obliged to have her "coming out".

She didn't know where her volume was; stuffed in a box somewhere, surely. Hers had been very dull—unless you were riveted by tips on how to throw the perfect luncheon party.

Still, she supposed it might be useful to her, under current circumstances. She'd have to check the chapters on how to address correspondence to various members of the peerage, and conventions of seating precedence. Such topics were bound to be included in a book of this sort.

Miss Abernathy's bag had turned out to be rather a let down—apart from the bar of Fry's. She stretched out her legs towards the stove, letting it warm the soles of her feet. Lady-like behaviour be damned. He already thought she smoked a pipe and secretly swigged spirits; a flash of ankle was hardly likely to make much difference. Besides which, once he'd delivered her to the castle, they'd never see each other again. He was charming in his way, but she didn't suppose his relatives mixed in the same circles as the laird.

It was probably for the best. He already knew too much about her. Once she reached Dunrannoch, she'd need to act her part far more thoroughly.

She'd put up her hair only hurriedly before going to the dining car that morning. With her rush to disembark the train, then the snow and everything that had happened, several strands at the back were falling down, and the rest had to be a mess. She took out the pins, running her fingers through to unsnag the tangles. It didn't help that her hair had gotten wet.

The room was warming up nicely though. Once dry, she'd curl it round her fist and pin it back into a bun at the nape of her neck.

"Here. Try a sip o' this." Rye had been busy while she perused the book. Both cups were filled to the brim. "There's a dash o' brandy to liven it up. Seein' as we might call this an emergency. Just sip it slow."

It smelt surprisingly good and the taste wasn't bad, with the hot water mixed in.

Ursula took another mouthful. The heat travelled downwards in a most pleasant way.

"You can call me Ursula, if you like."

Resolving to be nicer to him, she handed over a piece of chocolate. After all, he'd been true to his word. He hadn't tried to molest her. Rather, all his actions had been considerate.

From the deep recessed window, Ursula watched the whitewashed landscape fading to grey as the sun disappeared.

On the whole, it was a good thing they'd stumbled into one another. She might otherwise still be trudging through the snow, ending up who knew where.

CHAPTER SEVEN

A bothy, on Rannoch Moor
Early evening, 13th December

THERE WAS NO AVOIDING IT. They were stuck there, together in the bothy, until the mist lifted and the snow let up.

They ate the rest of the chocolate and drank more hot water laced with brandy. Though her head was a little fuzzy, she was feeling more at ease than she had in a long time.

It had grown dark, the only light coming from the wood burner.

He'd slipped outside for a while but was now settled cross-legged by their fire, looking as if he sat on the ground all the time.

Perhaps he did.

He nodded towards the door. "I checked on Charon— gave him some of our water. It's still snowing, thick n' heavy. No sign o' the moon."

She came to sit beside him. Not on the chair but on the floor, pulling her knees up to her chest and gathering her skirts close round her. Making more room, he scooted over, giving her the prime spot, right where the fire glowed hottest.

Clearing her throat, she said, "What is it you do, in Texas?"

He didn't answer right away, surveying her through half-closed eyes, as if weighing up how much she'd be interested in hearing.

"I work on a ranch with near ten thousand head o' Long-horn cattle. Three times a year, we drive a couple thousand to the railroad in San Antonio."

"That sounds like hard work."

"Yes, ma'am."

"But also quite exciting."

That smile; his mouth, quirking up on one side.

"There's nothin' like spending the night in the wide, wide open, with nothin' between you and the stars: Orion, Cassiopeia, Scorpius…and Ursa Minor, o' course. Named for you, lil bear."

Ursula hoped it was dark enough to conceal the flush creeping through her. It was his voice—that long, slow drawl. That and the way he was looking at her.

"You shouldn't call me that." She attempted a reproving look. "I'm Ursula or Miss Abernathy."

"I beg your pardon, ma'am." He tipped off his hat then settled it back, staring at her still from behind its rim.

He didn't look sorry.

He was laughing at her; she was certain of it, but she was determined to keep their conversation civil.

"What else do you miss?" she asked. "Your family I suppose."

Again, he took a moment before answering. "Most every-thin', truth be told—but my dog especially."

Her shoulders relaxed a smidge. Here was a subject they could talk of without her feeling awkward. She'd had a dachshund some years ago and had been thinking of purchasing another. Once she came into her money, she'd do just that. She could have five if she liked! There would be no one to say she couldn't.

The thought brought her a wave of pleasure.

Her current situation wasn't what she would choose, but it was an adventure of sorts, and it wouldn't be for long. Soon, she'd have the financial independence to make her own decisions.

"What breed is he, your dog?"

"A blue and tan Lacy." Rye gave her a genuine smile now —one that had nothing to do with teasing her. "Helps herd the livestock. He's smart as they come, and loyal with it."

"All dogs are loyal, aren't they?" Ursula sighed. "More reliable than people on the whole."

"It's like the story of Argos." Rye moved his weight to one side. "You know it, right? After twenty years o' his master wandering, he was the only one to recognize him."

He'd read *The Odyssey?* Of course, why shouldn't he? They had books in Texas, just like everywhere else.

Rye continued. "That poor dog'd been neglected all the time Odysseus was away. He was unloved, weak and full o' lice, but it dint stop him waggin' his tail on his master's return. He lacked even the strength to walk over to him, and Odysseus couldn't go to him for fear of discovery, but Argos showed he was loyal. Content at last, the old fella lay down and died, and Odysseus couldn't do anything but wipe away his tears—not wantin' his enemies to see and guess who he was."

Ursula couldn't help but notice that Rye's eyes were glistening.

"The bond between a dog and his master puts most human loyalties to shame," she said softly. Perhaps it was the firelight, or the brandy from before, but she felt softer alto-gether, as if she was letting go of something that had been wound tight inside.

"Same with horses." Rye nodded. "Take Charon there, the Hanovarian I was ridin'. He wouldn't look at anyone when I first came. Since he threw his master, no one's wanted anythin' to do with him. It's a shame, pure and simple, but Charon and I are gettin' along just fine. He's been starved of affection is all."

RYE LEANT FORWARD. The room had toasted up nicely but he opened the stove to add more fuel, poking at the embers to stir up the flames.

She was resting her chin on her knees, looking at him, her eyes wide; hazel green with amber flecks, and lashes tipped in gold. It had been her eyes he'd noticed first, when Charon had brought him near on top of her, almost knocking her down. They'd given each other a fright—no doubt about that.

He'd been foolish, setting out when he could see mist rolling down the hills. As he'd saddled the horse, Campbell had warned him against it, but he hadn't been able to face a whole day inside. There were too many women at Dunrannoch. He wasn't used to it—all that chatter about not much at all.

Lavinia hadn't laid it out for him explicitly but it was obvious what they had in mind, and he could hardly blame them. Dunrannoch was their home. It was only natural they'd want to safeguard their place in it. His grandfather was tenacious all right, but he wouldn't see out too many more years.

Rye had known the deal. Coming over here, taking on the mantle that could have been his father's, he'd a duty to continue the line—and that meant finding a wife.

Or being provisioned with one.

He'd only been at Dunrannoch a couple of weeks but, already, he was being backed into a corner. Not that they weren't amenable, those cousins of his: Fiona, Blair, Bonnie, Cora and Elspeth. All dark haired and blue-eyed and pretty as porcelain dolls. As far as he could tell, there wasn't much to choose between them. Perhaps that was the problem. It felt like picking a shirt from a whole pile stitched just the same.

Damn! He was an ungrateful son of a bitch.

Of course, he'd planned to settle down one day and raise a brood. He just hadn't realized it would happen so quickly. Any other fella would've been feeling like a kid in a confectionary shop; instead, he'd only been feeling trapped.

Until now.

Until Miss Ursula Abernathy, sitting there with her honeyed hair all loose about her shoulders, and those dainty bare feet, pale as milk. One long, thick ribbon of satin caramel curled down one side, reaching over the curve of her breast, all the way to her waist.

He'd a yearning to find out how soft it was but he'd made himself sit far enough away that he wouldn't overstep the boundaries. As it was, he'd have to spin a tale to keep her reputation intact.

He couldn't make out if she was flirting with him, with that velvety look in her eyes. When her nose wasn't wrinkling in disapproval, she sure was pretty.

He'd no idea what she was thinking right now.

Nor what she'd say when she worked out who he was.

He hadn't lied. Not exactly. He just hadn't wanted to tell her—not yet. In case it changed how she acted towards him.

And though he might not be telling Miss Ursula Abernathy the whole truth, he was darned sure she was holding a few things back herself.

They sat for a long while, drinking the last of the brandy, saying not much at all. Rye tried hard to keep himself from staring. She'd closed her eyes, tilting her head on one side.

Her lips were pale pink and petal-plump, parted in just the right way for kissing.

When riled, she was prickly as a cactus—but kissing her would smooth that out some. That, and holding her close, convincing her that she was safe—that nothing bad could reach her.

"You're tired, little bear." He pushed back a lock of hair from her cheek. "You should get to bed before y' tump over."

Drowsy, she opened one eye. "Where will you sleep?"

"Right here. I've slept on rougher ground. I'll be fine." Even as he said it, he was thinking of how he'd like to curl up behind her and tuck her into him. He wanted her close enough that he'd be able to smell her hair.

If he were honest, he wanted the roundedness of her behind pressed up against him too, but he shoved that thought away quickly. She trusted him, and he wouldn't do anything to make her regret that.

"Come on now." He got her under the arms, raising her up.

He shouldn't have given her the last tot of brandy. She wasn't used to liquor.

Reaching the wooden cot, she lay down at once, tucking her knees up. It couldn't be too comfortable; the horsehair mattress was losing its stuffing. He laid the rough blanket over her and she said nothing but, as he stepped away she reached out one arm, her fingers brushing his lower thigh.

"Keep me warm."

"You want me to hold you?" His voiced came out cracked. He knew it was a bad idea but God help him, he was only human.

She nodded and rolled over, leaving space for him. Not much, but just enough. If he turned in the night, he'd pitch right out and onto the floor.

He adjusted the blanket, making sure her feet were covered, then slipped alongside. He only hesitated a moment before putting his arm over her shoulder, making her snug in the crook.

The rest of him he kept apart from her, but she pushed back, as if by instinct, so that her thigh and her cold little feet sought his. Even through her numerous petticoats and layers, he could feel the warmest part of her, fleshy, rubbing against his groin.

He groaned.

Couldn't she feel it? The almighty cock-stand she'd given him?

Apparently, she could, for she sighed and wriggled, but then her breathing slowed.

The brandy sent her straight to sleep.

Rye smoothed her hair and moved up the bed a little. He couldn't help the erection in his breeches but he'd at least be gentlemanly enough to stick it into her back rather than the cleft of her buttocks.

It was a good hour before he drifted off, dreaming of wide-open plains and a horse saddled beneath him. He was riding hard, heading into the haze of the desert, towards something he couldn't quite make out. Something waiting for him in the far-off distance. Something, or someone.

CHAPTER EIGHT

Early morning, 14th December

Ursula woke shivering.

She was alone in the truckle bed and the fire had almost gone out, the embers in the stove glowing only dimly.

Where was he?

As she sat up, there was a horrible stabbing through her brain.

Good God!

She raised her hand to her forehead. It wasn't hot, or bleeding—just dizzy and sore. And her mouth seemed to be full of sand.

Oh for a cup of Earl Grey!

Gingerly, she lowered her toes to the floor. Someone—Rye of course—had draped her stockings of the day before at the end of the bed, and put her shoes nearby. Lowering her head to reach her feet brought on the jagged spike of pain so she leaned back, contorting herself to avoid further infliction.

Slowly, she stood up, taking small steps to the table, upon which her coat lay. It was dry, thank goodness.

He'd left a cup of water for her and, eagerly, Ursula drank it down, though its coldness made her shudder.

The addition of the liquid to her insides brought about a sudden awareness of her bladder and, heavens to goodness, there was no chamber pot! If she wanted to relieve herself, there was only the pan they'd used for boiling the snow—or she might manage with the cup.

She tried to gauge its capacity. No—it would have to be the pan; and best to do it quickly, before Rye came back.

Of course, he would be outside—perhaps answering the same call of nature, or seeing to the horse. It must be ravenous, poor thing. Although her stomach was jumping about, Ursula rather thought she was too. The chocolate hadn't gone far in filling her up and she'd had nothing else since breakfast on the train.

That thought brought an anxious tightening to her belly. Could she really go through with this? They'd have found Miss Abernathy before the train reached Fort William, surely. There might be a story in the newspapers. How long before something reached Dunrannoch and they discovered she was an imposter?

Ursula felt sick.

But it was all nonsense. Of course it wouldn't be in the papers. She hadn't been murdered. She was simply an elderly lady who'd passed away, quietly.

Ursula had only to keep her head. She'd been altogether silly to leave the train as she had. What had she been thinking? She might have been with Daphne by now.

But it was done, and here she was, and why shouldn't Dunrannoch be as good a place to hide-out as any. If she only kept a cool demeanour, she could pull off what was required.

It was certainly preferable to having stayed in London with her vile uncle.

Having utilized the pan, Ursula slipped on her coat. She'd

nip outside and empty her offering, then give it a rinse in the snow.

Opening the door, she was struck first by how dazzling the sky had become. The clouds had gone entirely, leaving an expanse of brilliant blue and, though still low on the horizon, the sun was shining brightly.

It was hard to believe the mist had ever existed.

The snow, however, was another matter. It must have long-since stopped falling but it lay deep outside—almost to her knees, and drifting deeper either side of the door. She could see where Rye had pushed his way through the powder, making a channel which led off to where he'd stabled the stallion.

Damn!

She could hardly throw the pan's contents from where she stood. He'd be bound to see the result. Unless she did so and then scooped some snow to cover over the tell-tale yellow.

As she was pondering the best approach, there was a deep, rumbling groan from just beyond the threshold—a lowing, throaty, bovine bray that concluded with the appearance of a huge, shaggy head in the doorway.

The pan seemed to leap from her hand at the same moment as she let forth an almighty scream. The monster, undeterred, pushed its nose forward.

Ursula screamed again, although more with surprise than horror. The beast was an alarming shade of orange and its horns were certainly fearsome, but it was only a cow.

"Out!" She shoved back against its wet snoot. "Off! Go! Skiddadle!"

"Ursula! You alright in there?" Rye's voice drifted over from somewhere behind the cow.

"Yes. Absolutely fine." She gritted her teeth.

"A grand dame of a critter, ain't she?" He gave the cow a slap across the behind, followed by another, making the creature turn its head and shamble round. Another prod and it shuffled off through the snow, lowing disconsolately.

When Rye came into view, he was holding the pan. "Were you throwing this?"

"Of course not! I was just…" She scowled. "It doesn't matter. Just give it to me!"

"Keep your petticoats straight." He gave her a grin. "We should move out while we can. Snow's too deep for them to send the carriage. Train'll be coming in about now anyways. We can say you came in on it and I found you waitin'. No-one'll be any the wiser that we spent a glorious night together."

"We did no such thing!" A flush of heat rose to Ursula's cheek

He raised his eyebrows. "You don't remember?"

Ursula frowned. She was certain nothing had happened but she'd been very sleepy. He'd promised to be gentlemanly, after all, and everything she'd seen of him so far seemed honourable.

"My apologies, Miss Abernathy." He must have realized her anxiety for he stepped forward and touched her shoulder. "I'm just teasin'. Your virtue's intact. I kept you warm; that's all."

"Of course." Ursula smoothed down her skirts and shrugged off his hand. "I knew that all along." Her tone was more clipped than necessary.

They'd overstepped boundaries in the forced intimacy of the night and, for that, Ursula blamed herself.

It might have been the pounding in her head, or the embarrassment she was feeling, or anxiety over what awaited her that day, but Ursula felt a hollow nausea as he helped her back onto the horse.

A FLOCK OF CROWS ROSE, cawing above Castle Dunrannoch.

It loomed sheer from the white expanse of the moor—a forbidding edifice of granite, its crenellated towers and sentry walks surrounding a central gate. Far off, to the north and west, mountains soared upward, snow-topped and formidable.

The castle didn't look as if it would have a great deal of comforts, and Daphne's warnings came to mind, of draughty corridors and fireplaces that refused to draw. Ursula could put up with many things, but she hated being cold. The idea of visiting Daphne at her own castle residence had seemed rather a lark. Gazing up at the fortress before her, Ursula felt altogether differently.

This was where she'd be spending the festive season—not in London, with the gaiety of shops and colourful street illuminations and every sort of fancy to tempt one. And not with her father.

No one here meant anything to her; nor she to them. It was a sorrowful thought.

Meanwhile, an awkwardness had fallen between her and Rye. He'd said barely a word as they'd drawn closer to the castle, passing through the snowy moorland landscape.

"I s'pose it'd be frowned upon for you to arrive at your new place of employ with my arms around you."

She couldn't see his face but he squeezed his elbows inward, making her aware of how closely she was tucked into his chest.

She nodded. It was good of him to think of it.

"I'll let you ride in while I walk beside." In a single, fluid motion Rye dismounted, taking the reins to lead Charon from ahead.

They entered under the iron portcullis, its spikes set high above the arching gate. Ursula almost expected it to come rattling down, some force having divined the false pretences under which she was invading these ancient walls, but none barred their way.

Someone had shovelled the snow into great piles, to leave the main courtyard accessible; Charon's hooves clattered loud upon the cobbles.

Rye guided the stallion towards the stables. "He's about ready for some hay. I'll see to him before…"

"Yes, of course. I'll be fine from here."

The fresh air had lifted Ursula's headache somewhat. She unhooked her feet from the stirrups and accepted his hands upon her waist, helping lift her down. He held onto her slightly longer than was necessary, looking at her mouth all the while. The bizarre thought came that he might kiss her and that, if he did, despite everything, she wouldn't stop him. But the moment passed and he stepped back.

Embarrassed, Ursula cleared her throat. "It was very nice to meet you." Without raising her eyes to his, she held out her hand for him to shake.

He gave a nervous laugh, giving her hand a gentle squeeze. "Likewise, Miss Abernathy—and I hope you'll forgive me…" His voice trailed off. His teasing demeanour had passed and he looked regretful.

A stable lad was already coming out to them.

It was time to part.

Ursula looked around the courtyard. While the exterior of the castle had arrow slits rather than true windows, the interior walls boasted tall panes of leaded glass. Anyone might be watching. She couldn't tell.

Already, they might have formed an unfavourable opinion of her, watching her and Rye together.

On the far side, a door opened and someone in staff uniform stood waiting for her.

"Goodbye then." She took the bags and turned her back.

It was time to become Miss Urania Abernathy.

CHAPTER NINE

Castle Dunrannoch
Mid-morning, 14th December

STAMPING HER FEET, Ursula shook off the snow.

"This way, Miss Abernathy." The housekeeper, Mrs. Douglas, did not smile; nor did she offer to help Ursula with her bags.

It was hardly the warmest of welcomes but, of course, she wasn't a guest in the traditional sense. She was a servant of sorts. Mrs. Douglas, no doubt, considered herself superior.

The corridor was most certainly for servants' use, being narrow and dark. Ursula followed behind. Mrs. Douglas' silvered hair had been pinned so tight into its bun, Ursula wondered how the older woman could bare it. It was some people's way though, she knew, to take pleasure in a little stoic suffering.

It appeared that electricity had yet to come to Castle Dunrannoch, for Mrs. Douglas carried a lantern. They made their way to the end of the passage and up a twisting stair, the lamplight revealing worn-down steps and rough stone walls. It was no easy task to carry her bags and ascend but, at last, they emerged onto an upper passageway.

"This is yours." Mrs. Douglas pushed open a door half-way along. Light filtered through three slim openings in the outer wall but only dimly, despite the bright sunshine of the day. They looked to be five feet thick, the slits deeply recessed.

No fire had been lit, though there was a basket of peat and some kindling. She'd have to see to that herself.

The chamber smelt damp but the bed looked comfortable —boxed on three sides and with a curtain for the side facing the room. Embroidered prettily with cruet flowers and inter-twining vines, it matched the coverlet. The single armchair, though it had seen better days, had been likewise adorned with an embroidered cushion. A wardrobe and table—upon which stood the customary pitcher and jug, were the only other furnishings.

"I'll wait while you tidy yourself." Mrs. Douglas gave a disapproving sniff. "The countess is in the morning room and will see you as soon as you're presentable. Don't take too long about it."

"Of course; thank you." She was aware of how rumpled she must look—her hair especially. Ursula reminded herself to smile. It wouldn't do to get on Mrs. Douglas' bad side.

Quickly, she changed into a skirt of plain green wool with matching jacket. With her hair repinned, she hoped she'd do.

Returning down the steeply spiralled stairs, they took a different direction at the bottom, stepping through into the cavernous hallway of the castle. The doorway they'd used was concealed within wooden panelling, becoming invisible once closed behind them. Here, the staircase was much grander, of the same dark oak, sweeping majestically to a half-landing before splitting off to either side.

The ceiling, high above, was similarly panelled, while the walls were covered with dusty tapestries, their threads coming loose along lower edges. The floor was cold flag-stone, devoid even of a rug. From the far side, Ursula heard conversation. Someone laughing.

That was more like it. Not everything in the castle could be veiled in dismal gloom.

Mrs. Douglas opened the door and ushered her through.

The woman who rose to greet her was undoubtedly the countess. Though it was barely eleven in the morning, Lady Dunrannoch was resplendently dressed in purple silk, with ruffles of black lace at her neck and cuffs. Expertly coiffed, her pure white hair was set off by droplet jet earrings. She cut a striking figure. Clearly, she'd been a great beauty in her time, carrying herself with the bearing of one accustomed to admiration.

The room meanwhile, bore none of the austerity of the entranceway. Here were signs of the Yuletide season, for wreaths of bright-berried holly and twining ivy, spruce and pine swagged the rafters and mantlepiece.

A huge fireplace filled a portion of the inner wall, its grate stacked high and producing a considerable amount of heat, before which lay a rather despondent looking wolfhound, its head down on the rug.

Every available section of wood panelling had been adorned with the head of a stag, and there were perhaps fifty in all, encircling the room, looking down on the assembled women of the family, the faces of whom were turned to appraise the newcomer.

Lady Dunrannoch inclined her head, peering at Ursula with slight puzzlement before collecting herself to make introductions and Ursula found herself obliged to drop multiple curtsies.

"The Dowager Countess," began Lady Dunrannoch.

Of most ancient years, the lady in question—hunched in her chair and wearing a dress out of fashion these forty years

—gawked beadily at Ursula before returning her attention to a plate of cake upon her lap.

"Lady Arabella Balmore and Lady Mary Balmore—widows to my dearly departed step-sons, and my step-daughter, Lady Iona." They stared at Ursula with interest, the two Lady Balmores sharing a furtive glance with eyebrows arched.

"And my five granddaughters, Ladies Fiona, Bonnie, Cora, Elsbeth and Blair." The young ladies varied in age from perhaps sixteen to twenty.

"Lady Iona's son, Cameron, is attending to business in Pitlochrie but you'll meet him soon. The earl, sadly, is recovering from a head cold and confined to his room at present."

"Do have a seat, Miss Abernathy." The countess indicated a space on the sofa opposite, upon which was a liberal sprinkling of orange hair.

The ginger cat sitting at the countess's feet paused from licking its paw to give Ursula a look of disdain.

"Some tea? I expect you're gasping for a cup after your arduous journey. Really most kind of you to come at such short notice."

The countess turned to the maid standing to one side. "More hot water, Winnie." She waved her hand at the platters set upon various tables about the room. "And shortbread. See if Mrs. Middymuckle has any of her drop scones for us, if you please."

"Thank you." Ursula accepted a mince pie. Being quite ravenous, she took a large bite but, brimming with hot sultanas, it burnt her mouth, causing her to splutter.

Two of the younger girls tittered.

Lady Dunrannoch merely added a lump of sugar to her own cup and stirred vigorously.

"I hope you won't be too uncomfortable here, Miss Abernathy. We're rather lacking in modern conveniences—still using oil lamps and candles, since we haven't the electricity here. There's no telephone of course, though we go to town every few weeks or so. You can post letters from there, or send a telegram."

Producing a sardine from her sandwich, she reached down to offer it to the cat, who accepted with utmost daintiness, its sharp, white teeth closing around the morsel.

"McTavish has a delicate constitution." The countess beamed down at the generously proportioned cat, now wiping its whiskers on her skirts.

She gave a tinkling laugh.

"It was a condition of my marrying the earl that he have decent plumbing installed, so we don't want for hot water, at least. Apart from that, Castle Dunrannoch is little changed since the days of Robert the Bruce. He's said to have stayed here, you know, in 1306, shortly before his crowning."

The dowager stirred, looking up from her fruit cake. Her voice rang out with remarkable force, her eyes suddenly blazing. "Hosted by Camdyn Dalreagh, the Wolf of Dunrannoch, whose ghost walks among us still." She leant forward, her gnarled fingers grasping the armrest of her seat. "The curse is upon us! Beware the bagpipes! Each clansman shall meet his death!"

"Now, now, Flora! Enough of that." The countess patted the old woman's hand, then turned to Ursula with apologetic eyes. "The dowager sees the supernatural in everything. Of course, there's no denying that the castle has a grisly history —bodies holed up in the walls and what have you, but there's a chair on the upper passageway that she declares is possessed by the spirit of her old Pekinese. She leaves out a tidbit on the cushion every night and swears blind it's the spectral visitation that polishes it off."

McTavish stretched and yawned, then leapt to sit on the Countess' lap, looking decidedly smug.

"As for the curse, it's all nonsense. Lyle McDoon, being a lecherous old reprobate, was refused the hand of Camdyn's youngest daughter, and vowed that every male heir of the Dalreagh line would perish an untimely death." She rubbed McTavish's ears. "Of course, 'untimely' is a bit vague. The earl is nearly eighty, after all. As for the bagpipes, it's said that Camdyn plays them on the battlements on the eve of one of the clansmen meeting his end."

She looked over at the Lady Balmores, both of whom were looking rather pale. "Forgive me, my dears. A sensitive subject, I know."

"Now, Miss Abernathy." She turned again to Ursula. "I must say that you're considerably younger than I was led to believe. Lady Forres indicated that you'd many years' experience."

"Ah well. Actually, I'm thirty-eight. I just look rather younger." Ursula bit her lip. Truly, God would strike her down for the lies she was telling. A bolt of lightning was sure to come down the chimney and smite her on the spot.

"Goodness me!" exclaimed the Countess. "Another day, you must tell us your secret."

With eyes downcast, Ursula selected a liver paste sandwich. She'd save some ash from the fire and draw on a few wrinkles before she next joined the family.

"And what an unusual accent you have, Miss Abernathy. Which part of Scotland did you say you're from?"

Ursula gave a nervous laugh. "Oh, my accent?"

Clearing her throat, she emulated the rhythms of the countess' own gentle lilt. "It comes and goes. For my work, you see, I need to soften my native brogue. Our seat is to the south but I haven't ever lived there. My father having married against the wishes of his family, we've moved about rather a lot."

"Ah, a love match." The countess nodded. "Such as between the earl and myself. Second marriages are advantageous in that respect, though our union came too late for me to provide dear Dunrannoch with more children. A man may remain virile to the end, but we ladies ripen younger on the vine."

She looked wistfully towards the fire. "Fortunately, Dunrannoch married me without expectation of our passion bearing fruit."

One of the Lady Balmores coughed loudly and offered Ursula the plate of macaroons. "I believe you were most recently with Baron McBhinnie, of the Kilmarnock McBhinnies? A most respected family."

Ursula felt the colour rising to her cheeks. She really must guide the conversation onto something through which she could weave some semblance of the truth. "Ah yes, the McBhinnies! But it was my previous family that I vouch to know best—the Surrey Arringtons. Three young ladies all most keen on music and riding."

"Indeed." Lady Balmore eyed Ursula over the rim of her teacup, looking as if she didn't believe a word of it.

The countess cast her eyes over the assembled party. "My darlings, if you've finished, might I have some time alone with our guest? Fiona and Bonnie, would you escort your great-grandmother back to her room. And, Cora, perhaps you'll find young Lord Balmore and ask him to join us. I must introduce him to Miss Abernathy, and we can discuss her various duties together."

With a flurry of skirts and cups clicked upon saucers, the room emptied, so that Ursula was soon alone with Lady Dunrannoch.

The countess set down McTavish and moved to take the seat next to her.

She spoke in a confidential tone. "I want to confide in you Miss Abernathy, to ensure you appreciate the unusual nature of our situation."

She passed her hand over her forehead. "I'd almost given up hope of us finding the earl's third son, Rory. It was a day of sadness when I received the telegram informing me of his passing. But one of joy also, since it contained news that his son would take his rightful place in this family. The Dalreaghs have lost so much—" She broke off, her eyes glistening. "Brodie and Lachlan—they weren't my own, but I helped raise them. Their deaths have been so hard for us to bear."

Pulling out a handkerchief, she dabbed at her eyes. "I'm sure you can see the way of things. I have five granddaughters, Miss Abernathy, and I'm eager to arrange a betrothal to our new Lord Balmore. It may seem a hasty desire, and marriage to one's cousin is not as usual as it once was, but I feel we should waste no time."

Ursula was rather taken aback.

Does she intend the child to make a promise of betrothal to one of those girls? Could such a thing be binding?

The countess sat a little more upright in her chair, assuming a more businesslike manner. "The young fellow has great potential, but his manners are lacking. He is, without doubt, a Dalreagh, but he lacks the necessary refinement. I wish to rectify this in time for our festive cèilidh, and shall be encouraging him to make his choice on that very night. You'll do all you can, I hope, to ensure a smooth transition for him."

Ursula could not hide her surprise. It all seemed highly irregular.

At that moment, the door opened.

"Ah, and here he is! Our darling boy!" declared the countess.

Ursula twisted round to cast eyes upon her charge and almost choked on her own tongue.

The man standing before her was no child, nor a gangling adolescent. He was tall and broad-shouldered. His hair was far longer than was fashionable for a gentleman, thick and curling at his collar and, though he'd changed his clothes, he'd not yet shaved, the stubble dark on his jaw.

Moreover, he wore no jacket, no waistcoat, nor a tie—only a linen shirt and moleskin breeches, the bulge of muscle evident on his upper arm and thigh.

To her horror, Ursula found that her pulse was racing.

His eyes twinkled as he walked towards them. He gave his grandmother a kiss upon the cheek and bestowed another on Ursula's hand.

"Well, Miss Abernathy." His lips curved in a half-smile. "It's a true delight to have you here."

CHAPTER TEN

Midday, 14th December

URSULA ROLLED up her clothes and shoved them back into her luggage. Her mind was made up. She wouldn't stay another moment.

She'd had to sit there, listening to Lady Dunrannoch detail her duties, while Rye—or Lord Balmore as she was now supposed to address him—gave her that brash smile, his eyes crinkling up, no doubt having a good laugh at her expense.

The story he'd told her in the bothy hadn't exactly been untrue of course, but he'd omitted all the salient details—and he'd let her ramble on, digging herself into an embarrassing hole.

The situation was insufferable.

She needed only to return to the platform and wave down the next train to pass through, reverting to her original plan of visiting Daphne. There must be several through the day, surely?

With a sigh, she sat on the edge of the bed. Impulsiveness had gotten her into this mess; perhaps it would be wise to wait until the next morning—at least she knew the time the early train crossed the moor, and the light seemed to be fading already, despite it being only midday.

Ursula passed her hand over her forehead. She hadn't intended for everything to become so complicated. Most certainly, it would have been better if she'd never met Miss Abernathy.

One thing was for sure; she had no intention of carrying her bag again. She'd give it to Mrs. Douglas and leave her to distribute the contents.

It was the sensible thing to do but the thought of it made Ursula feel callous. Miss Abernathy had been kind, truly. Pulling the bag onto the bed, Ursula unsnapped the clasp. Perhaps she'd keep something as a token. Her hand fell on the flask that had contained the brandy and she took a sniff.

Had it only been last night? She'd enjoyed hearing his stories, then sitting in companionable silence, watching the flickering of the fire. Later, the comfort of him curled to her back, his arm across her chest.

She threw the empty flask back into the bag.

It didn't change anything.

He was still insufferable.

And then, there it was again—the book: *The Lady's Guide to All Things Useful.* The flyleaf bore an inscription: *To my darling Urania, from your ever-loving sister, Violet — December 25th, 1855.*

The sister on the Dorset coast.

Would they have managed to contact her yet? To let her know that Urania had passed away? Probably not. They'd have been able to identify Miss Abernathy from the booking name on her overnight compartment but there mightn't be anything else among her possessions to even indicate she had a sister.

As it was, there was no address book in Urania's handbag. No doubt, she knew any address of importance by heart. She,

Ursula, would have to take the initiative. She wasn't sure how, as yet, but she'd find a way. There couldn't be too many women by the name of Violet Abernathy living along that piece of coastline.

She'd write, letting Violet know that Urania had been thinking of her.

Ursula flipped through the pages: recipes, cures for ailments, rules of etiquette, and the usual pithy nuggets of advice.

The chapter on "Honesty" fell open, as if it had been often called upon.

To thine own self be true, as the great philosophers say. However, a lady knows when she must speak the truth and when diplomacy is the better course of action. Gifts should be professed to be exactly what one would wish, and a friend should be complimented on any achievement with which she is clearly pleased herself. Our own opinion need not unfailingly be expressed, to spare the feelings of others.

In most matters, nonetheless, honesty should be observed in more than spirit. To tell falsehoods may seem expedient but they are likely to trip one up, and to cause more difficulty in the long run.

Well, Ursula could hardly argue with that.

While Rye had been frugal with the truth, she'd hardly been liberal with it herself. And the tales she'd spun Lady Dunrannoch; if she stayed, it would be all she could do to keep those straight.

She'd keep the book. Perhaps, she might send it on to Violet—if she managed to locate her place of residence.

Her thoughts were interrupted by a rap on the door and, before she had the chance to rise, the heavy oak pushed open.

"You!" Ursula leapt to her feet.

The person standing in her doorway, having to bend to avoid the upper lintel, was none other than Rye himself.

"I've come to apologize." He had the decency to look sheepish, at least. "I mean to say, there are things I should've mentioned."

Ursula felt a surge of anger. She'd had enough of being told half-truths. "You shouldn't be here. I'm only 'staff' but I still have a reputation. Did anyone see you come up?"

"But I'm only—" He looked confused for a moment then shook his head. "No. No one knows I'm here."

"That's something." She barged past him to close the door then stood with her back to it.

Rye turned to face her. "I knew I ought to tell you, but I never could find the right moment."

Ursula folded her arms. "I'm sure it was far too amusing, having me ranting on. Why would you want to stop me?"

"It wasn't like that, Ursula." He pushed his fingers through his hair. "You made me laugh, sure, but I wasn't laughing 'at' you."

The look he gave her was earnest. In her heart, she knew he was telling the truth but her pride remained wounded.

"Since I won't be staying, it doesn't matter." She stepped to one side, grasping the door handle. "I took the position on a whim and it was a mistake. If there's a cart or something to take me, I'll depart tomorrow. Now, I think you should leave."

"Whoa there." In one stride, he was in front of her, his palms on her shoulders. She was brought up short, confronted by the sheer physicality of him, smelling faintly of perspiration and sandalwood—more strongly of horse and leather and peat smoke. And his hands were so warm. She remembered how it had felt to have him lie beside her through the night, how it had felt to have him hold her while they were riding.

"There's no need for you to go anywhere. We can forget all this, can't we? Move past it; start again?"

She didn't know why he was making such a fuss. It couldn't matter whether she stayed. There were enough other people to show him the things they were expecting her to teach him.

Part of her wanted to agree to anything he asked. The way he was holding onto her made it difficult to think of leaving, but she shook her head. "You weren't completely honest with me—"

He interrupted her before she could finish. "And you're telling me that you have been?"

"I d-don't know what you mean." Ursula looked upward, into eyes that told her he wasn't fooled.

"Well, Miss Abernathy, I can't say that I understand what's going on here, but somethin' doesn't quite add up— what with you thinkin' you were comin' up here to teach a child."

"A simple misunderstanding." Ursula shrugged away from Rye's hold. "I was distracted when the initial letter of request arrived. There's nothing more to it."

"Uh huh?" Rye folded his arms. "So why is it I get the feelin' you're running away from somethin'?"

"Running away?" Ursula frowned. "Don't be ridiculous. I came here to do a job."

"And what's with the accent you're usin' with my grandmother?"

Ursula had no answer for that—or none she cared to share with him.

He raised one eyebrow. "Look, I'll be honest with you. Then you can decide how honest you want to be with me."

"If you must." Mrs. Douglas was sending up some lunch on a tray at one o'clock. She'd just need to be sure Rye was gone before then. Meanwhile, she might as well warm up the room. Bending to the grate, she fiddled with bits of kindling, only to find him kneeling next to her.

"I promised my father and I'm determined to see it through. I'll be learnin' everything about the cattle 'n' the estate. I'll take good care of the folks that rely on this place for their livelihood and—"

"—you'll wed as your family see fit."

"A wife will keep me on the straight and narrow, I guess." Rye shrugged.

And put the necessary babies in the nursery for you. Ursula snapped a twig in two, throwing it on top of the others.

"It's not how I imagined doing things, but they're stuck with me, and I'm not what they were expecting. I need to make a few concessions."

"But you've left behind everything you grew up with to come here. Isn't that enough?" She sat back on her heels, glaring at him. If she felt indignant about it, why didn't he?

"I told you, little bear; I've promises to keep." He looked suddenly weary.

"And five young women lined up to flutter their lashes at you!" The words were out before Ursula had the chance to catch them. She bit her lip. He'd be thinking she was jealous, which was ridiculous. She'd only met him the day before; they didn't know each other.

Neither did his girl cousins, of course, but that wasn't going to stop him from marrying one of them.

"And I'll be the one doin' the choosing." He spoke softly.

"That's what they want you to think." She picked up a larger piece of kindling, attempting to break it over her knee. "They don't know the first thing about you. They employed someone to make you fit in. Doesn't that irritate you?" After several failed attempts she threw the wood aside, sucking at her thumb.

They'll polish down your rough edges to turn you into something they think acceptable. They'll dictate your clothes and manners and change your accent if they can—that honeyed drawl that's part of who you are. And they'll marry you to their own to keep everything within the status quo.

"I need you, Ursula. I need you to help me, so that I can do what's right." He brought his hand over hers. "Show me what it is they're expectin' and I'll do my darndest not to let them down."

What other people were expecting? He was right that she was on the run—and it was other people's expectations she was running from.

Yet here he was, running towards them.

His situation, of course, was different from her own. Ultimately, he'd have charge of his destiny in a way she never would.

She pulled her hand out from beneath his and brought it to her lap. He didn't need to know how she'd ended up here, nor what she planned for her own future, but she could give him a few days.

"All right. I'll stay." She rubbed at the splinter in the pad of her thumb, keeping her eyes down. "But don't ask me anything else."

Leaving, he paused on the threshold and she glanced up then, but he was only checking that the passage was clear.

He didn't look round again but she heard him as the door clicked shut.

"Fair enough, little bear."

CHAPTER ELEVEN

Early-afternoon, 15th December

BLACKENED WITH CENTURIES OF SOOT, the vaulted rafters of Dunrannoch's banqueting hall stretched high above, leading the eye to a minstrels' galley occupying one end, large enough to accommodate a small orchestra.

It wasn't hard to imagine a gathering. The room had been built for that purpose—to bring together every member of the household in communal festivity. The cavernous fireplace would have blazed high, while long tables and benches would have filled its length and the hall would have resonated with the chatter of several hundred voices.

Now, the emptiness echoed.

In preparation for the Yuletide cèilidh, the staff of Dunrannoch had begun to hang greenery and a small fire had been set at one end of the hearth, producing a modicum of warmth to supplement the cool winter light entering through the hall's windows of leaded glass.

It was here that Ursula was to teach Lord Balmore the deportment required of a gentleman. So far, they'd addressed the conventions of cutlery and glassware, as well as various other table etiquette—from how to use a finger bowl to the correct manner in which to pass a bottle of port. Where Ursula had been unable to recall the details herself, Miss Abernathy's little guide had lived up to its title.

After a luncheon of venison pie, a hurried conference with MacBain, the butler, had apprised Ursula of the customary toasts of Burns' Night, and other festive occasions unique to the Scots. She'd located a volume of poetry by the great man for Rye to study at his leisure.

Ursula entered the banqueting hall to find him already waiting, bending over something on a side table. As he did so, his shirt pulled tight across his back. His physique spoke of his working life, there was no doubt about that, and he'd rolled up the cuffs of his shirt to his forearms—as if to take up a scythe, or manhandle a sheep for dipping. She hadn't forgotten how easily he'd lifted her, helping her into the saddle and out of it the day before.

It seemed that someone had brought in a gramophone and he was leafing through a stack of recordings—frowning at some, peering at the typeface upon others. She observed him remove one from its case and place it upon the turntable, winding the handle upon the side before lowering the needle. The shrill, wailing drone that emerged had him jumping back in horror.

Ursula rushed forward to lift the needle.

"Bagpipes." She held up the case, indicating the picture upon the front. "They're good for accompanying the Highland Fling and such—country dances, you know." She moved her feet in the semblance of a jig, to demonstrate. "But the clans used them for centuries in battle, since you could hear them over the din of all the fighting."

"No kidding." Rye shook his head. "I don't know how anyone's meant to dance to this. More like a bag o' wildcats fightin' each other than any music I ever heard."

"It's all part of your heritage."

"Are you ribbin' me, Miss Abernathy?" Rye cocked an eyebrow.

"Certainly not, Lord Balmore."

"Call me Rye, please; you know that's m'name."

Removing the offending bagpipes, she flipped through the other recordings, selecting an alternative. "You'll have to get used to it. Officially, everyone will refer to you as Balmore from now on—or Dunrannoch, when you come into your grandfather's title."

Rye frowned. "I don't know if I'll ever get used t'that."

As the first strains of the music rose, she directed him into position, placing his right hand on her waist. "That's what this is all about, isn't it? Helping you get used to new things. Now, I'm going to teach you to waltz, your lordship." She placed one hand in his, and her other on his upper arm— an appendage, she noted, that was hard with muscle.

With a grin, he wrapped her more firmly. "If it means holdin' you like this, I've no objection."

For a moment, she wanted only to remain still and savour how close they were standing; the way his arm was encircling her.

His fingers crept round farther, and he was staring hard into her eyes. He wasn't just teasing. She felt the force of something altogether more powerful. She'd never felt like this before, but she had an inkling of what it was.

The fluttering of her pulse might have made her think she was falling in love—or some such ridiculous notion—but she wasn't a ninny. They'd only just met. No one fell in love overnight.

This was physical attraction, pure and simple; some animal craving for which she was hardwired as much as he was.

She might have limited experience—that was to say, almost none—but her father had given her full reign over his library. Defoe's *Moll Flanders* had taught her a good deal.

Determined to remain in charge, she pushed away. "You aren't throwing me in the hay—or whatever it is you usually do with women. You need to maintain a respectable distance."

Rye wiggled his eyebrows but did just as he was told, creating the requisite space between them. "Yes, ma'am. Rules are rules. Can't have us forgettin' them and goin' wild."

Going wild? She couldn't begin to imagine; and now certainly wasn't the time.

She cleared her throat, and fixed her gaze somewhere around his clavicle. Everything would go easier if she avoided looking him directly in the eye.

"The waltz from *Swan Lake*—by Tchaikovsky. The idea is to float around the floor, in a fluid and elegant manner, moving in waves to the count of three. It's really very simple when you get the hang of it." For the next few minutes, she made him follow her feet. "Step and lean, and slide and rise. That's it—as if you're making a repeating box with your feet. Anti-clockwise around the room, making small extra turns as we go."

He grasped quickly all that she showed him. By the time she'd given the gramophone a fifth cranking, they were twirling at full speed. Really, it was quite wonderful. Rye seemed to be a natural, for all he'd never tried before.

She'd danced with any number of men during her season and none had made her feel like this—as if she could stay in their arms for hours, letting them spin her in circle after circle, to music rising and swelling.

As the waltz came to its crashing, tumultuous conclusion, he brought her to a stop by the window, both of them a little short-winded and laughing with pleasure.

"You did—very well." Ursula beamed, catching her breath.

He offered a bow to her curtsey and another of his grins. "You're an excellent teacher."

"Thank you." She was surprised at how much satisfaction

it gave her to hear his praise. "Of course, there's a lot more to learn yet. For instance, you shouldn't dance more than once with the same lady, unless you wish to show particular favour."

He'd suddenly stepped closer again. "And here we are, turning about the room over and over."

"Yes, well…it's perfectly acceptable while you're learning."

"Is that so?"

The way he said it, his drawling voice low in her ear, made it sound anything but.

Remember, it doesn't mean a thing. He has five would-be brides waiting in the wings, and you're nothing at all—just the hired help. Good enough for a quick squeeze, but don't fool yourself into thinking it means anything else.

Shaking her head clear, she went to pour them some water.

On her return, he was looking upward at a bunch at mistletoe hanging in the alcove.

"It has sacred powers you know." Ursula handed him his glass. "The old Druids used it in their ceremonies, thousands of years ago, and this time of year was when the plant was said to be most potent."

"Interesting." Rye drank down the water and craned his neck. "Potent for what exactly?"

"Healing illness, protecting against nightmares; predicting the future, even." Hurriedly, she relieved him of his glass, setting both on the little seat under the window.

She happened to know that the ancient Greeks had gathered mistletoe as well—for their festival of Saturnalia and for marriage ceremonies—because of its association with fertility, but she wasn't about to discuss that.

He reached up, plucking one white berry off the sprig.

"You shouldn't; it's unlucky just to pull them off. The only way to remedy it is to…" She paused, suddenly embarrassed. She'd been about to—almost had—invited him to kiss her!

"What's that, Miss Abernathy?" He bent down, so that his lips almost brushed her ear. "Is there somethin' else I need to know?"

IT WAS BAD OF HIM, he knew, teasing her like this, but it was too darn fun to resist.

He'd been a perfect gentleman, just as he'd promised, but there was a time for a man to show a woman what he was feeling—regardless of propriety.

And he'd been waiting all day for this, watching that sweet mouth of hers as she explained a hundred and one things he could barely see the reason for. It was all to make other people feel comfortable, she'd said, as well as setting an example—but he couldn't see the tenant farmers caring if he knew which fork was right for eating fish, or how he should be handling his napkin.

There was something else he did care about, and that was letting her know she was the best thing to have happened to him since he'd landed in this goddam place. He'd no idea if she'd been kissed before. It was hard to tell. She was all sorts of feisty but innocent with it: the way her face lit up when she laughed, and how the blush came roaring every time he brushed his fingers against hers.

But there was something mischievous, too—and not altogether ladylike, for someone who was supposed to be a teacher of etiquette.

As to whether she wanted him to kiss her, there was only one way to find out and that was to take the initiative. He'd cup his palm to that peach of a cheek and graze his lips against hers—going gently, of course.

She'd have the chance to get all indignant and stop him, if that was what she wanted. He only hoped he'd read the signs right, for once he started kissing her, he'd an idea it was going to be damn hard to stop.

They were already standing near hip to hip, so it was easy as pie to slide an arm back around her waist.

He surprised her alright, going by the gasp she gave as he pulled her in, but he'd been right about her being ready for kissing.

He let their lips touch just a little, to get acquainted, and she sighed right into his mouth. Tugging those petal-soft lips with his own, he had her arching into him. And, when he ran his tongue inside, she opened right up. She wasn't fighting him and she wasn't prickly. She was pliant and willing and pressing close.

She was trembling in all the right ways and kissing him back as if it were the only thing she wanted.

There was nothing about Miss Ursula Abernathy that was telling him to stop. On the contrary; she was waving a big old flag emblazoned with the word "go".

Deepening the kiss, he remembered what it had felt like to lie beside her all night, to feel her warmth and listen to her breathing. That scent of hers, too—talcum powder and roses, and a little hint of something musky.

He groaned with the pleasure of it and clasped her tighter, thinking about the whole damn sweetness of what she was offering.

A woman didn't melt like this unless she wanted a man to make love to her.

Yes, sir.

Miss Abernathy might talk of propriety but she was brimful of passion—and he was the lucky man to have discovered it before she even realized the fact herself.

CHAPTER TWELVE

Early-evening, 16th December

ALL NIGHT, she'd tossed in her bed, thinking about Rye Dalreagh.

Thinking about that head-spinningly delicious kiss, and how good it had felt, being embraced by all that manliness.

She was pretty certain that one, if not both, of his hands had somehow ended up cupping her bottom. There may even have been a moment in which he'd pushed his thigh between hers and, rather than slapping his face, she'd let him do it!

To top it all, she knew she'd pulled out the back of his shirt—with the sole intent of laying hands on his bare skin.

She was a hussy!

A brazen strumpet!

A jezebel in the making!

She was also an utter idiot. Because the kiss hadn't meant anything; none of it had.

When they'd come up for air, he'd gasped, "I don't think we should—" and then the female contingent of his family had squawked into the room.

Fortunately, at least, it seemed her floozy-like display had gone unwitnessed. If the countess had an inkling of Ursula's carnal proclivities, wouldn't she be thrown out on her ear? As it was, she'd merely summoned Ursula to the gramophone and asked her to get it going again, so that Rye might show them all he'd been learning.

All he'd been learning!

She'd been forced to stand and watch while his five cousins took him for a spin and, clearly, Ursula wasn't alone in harbouring shameless tendencies. Hers were not the only eyes admiring Lord Balmore's buttocks as he executed his turns. The women were like cats licking their chops over a particularly juicy bit of fillet.

Declaring herself delighted, the countess had promised they'd assemble again the following morning to teach him some cèilidh dances—those Scottish jigs in which you swapped partners at every corner and most of the places in between.

Rye had gone along with it all, and she could hardly blame him. He'd told her all about his idea of duty—of his intention to live up to his family's expectations and marry as they directed. It was only a waiting game.

Her lips—and other tender parts—had been nothing more than an *hors d'oeuvre*.

Come the afternoon, young Cameron had returned and whisked Rye off to discuss some new treatment for removing ticks from cattle—or something equally revolting—leaving Ursula to her own devices.

Retiring to her room, she'd brooded in maidenly frustration, wondering for the forty-seventh time what she was doing at Castle Dunrannoch. Even settling to a book seemed troublesome. What would Miss Abernathy have advised? To have her fun before the clock chimed midnight, or to pull herself together and behave with dignity?

She pulled out the little book again—*The Lady's Guide to*

All Things Useful. It had some queerly titled chapters, broaching subjects she would hardly have expected.

Flicking through, Ursula alighted on something about husbands, then seduction. Did the two go together? Surely, you didn't need to worry about seducing your own husband? There was some old wives' rubbish on aphrodisiacs and how to prevent pregnancy. Ursula gave a snort of derision but, on further consideration, made a small fold at the corner.

She scanned down the pages and her eye alighted on the word "lust". That was more like it. What was one supposed to do when in the throes of some unreasonable passion? Take up cold baths and knitting? Pray for guidance?

To lust is to desire without rational limit. It is a headstrong, galloping beast which marks not the rein. A craving of the blood for the forbidden. A darkness most alluring when the stakes are high. To lust is to lose oneself, but to find something, too—that part of us which wishes to tear at life and devour it. Without passion, what are we?

All things in moderation, as the adage goes—including moderation itself. There is a time for recklessness and the unbridling of desire. Only choose well the object of your cravings, and remember that bright flames are apt to quickest burn.

Well, that was a surprise. Ursula read the section a second time. These sorts of books didn't generally encourage one to give in to anything sinful.

Perhaps, with her time at Castle Dunrannoch being so short, she'd better get started on a little of that devouring, before Lord Balmore was permanently apportioned to someone else's plate.

The notion of normalcy had departed when she'd boarded the Caledonian Express, so she might as well embrace it and behave like a true adventuress.

As a starting point, she needed to dress for dinner. She'd

been so irked the previous evening that she'd pleaded a bad head and taken a tray in her room, but the countess was adamant she join them tonight, and the gong wouldn't be far off.

Ursula only hoped she'd remember everyone's names correctly, and how they were all related. There were so many generations and step-children…and how many Lady Balmores were there? It was tricky keeping it all straight. She'd quizzed the maid who'd brought her hot water, but there were still some gaps in her understanding.

Taking a piece of writing paper, she began jotting down all she could remember. She'd pop the mnemonic in her reticule and could take a peep if things got too confusing.

Rufus Dalreagh m. Flora (now dowager countess)

Laird Finlay Dalreagh ———————————2nd marriage to Lavinia
Earl of Dunrannoch   (Countess Dunrannoch)
(first wife died young?)

Brodie ————————————— Lachlan ———————————— Rory——————— Iona
(was Viscount Balmore)   (m. Mary - also Lady Balmore)   (m. someone unsuitable?)   (husband dead?)
(m. Arabella – first Lady Balmore)

Fiona   Bonnie — Cora — Elsbeth—Blair   Rye   Cameron

Certainly, there were no difficulties in choosing what to wear, for the restrictions of her luggage had permitted Ursula to pack only one change of skirt and jacket, three shirtwaists, and a single evening gown—one of dark blue silk with a low-scooped neck, embellished finely with midnight lace. She'd been confident that Daphne would lend her anything else she needed.

Still, the dress was flattering. She might sit at the Dalreagh table without feeling too humble.

Having contorted herself with the rear buttons, Ursula had begun pinning her hair—sighing for the absence of Tilly to help her—when there was a scratching at the door.

She pulled it open a crack and heard a faint feline mewl.

A small but determined paw pushed the door wider and McTavish manoeuvred himself inside. Brushing past Ursula's legs, he made a leap for the bed, stalking over the nightgown she'd laid out for warming, and settling himself bottom-first against her pillow.

She noticed then that he'd something in his mouth.

Something limp and scrawny, and very much dead.

With a satisfied air, McTavish deposited it on the coverlet.

"Urgh!" Ursula made no bones about shooing out the cat, closing the door firmly against McTavish's protests.

Bringing the oil lamp closer, she peered at the thing on the bed—a scrap of brown fur damp with feline drool, four tiny paws pointing ceiling-ward and a very long tail.

What was she to do with it? She might move the corpse to the peat basket and ask one of the maids to remove it for her. Certainly, she didn't intend to leave it where it was.

She was just reaching for the tail, when the mouse leapt up and burrowed under her nightdress.

Ursula gave more than a squeak!

The mouse, meanwhile, was quivering in fright, its whole body trembling.

"Oh dear," said Ursula. "You were only pretending—and now what shall I do with you?"

The mouse looked back at her with beady eyes, twitching its nose between layers of ribbon and lace. It was quite a pretty mouse, truly, with soft little ears.

"You need to go outside." Making herself brave, she scooped it up and went to the window.

That was no use at all. The glass didn't open. Besides which, it was simply too cruel. She could hardly throw the poor thing from the fourth floor. It had suffered quite enough.

With a sigh, she put it in her reticule. Downstairs, she'd release it from the outer doors.

CHAPTER THIRTEEN

A little later in the evening, 16th December

THE PORTRAIT DOMINATED the far wall—a devastatingly attractive man in full kilted regalia, complete with cascading lace ruffles on his shirt and glinting broadsword in hand. He'd the same dark, curling hair and chiselled jaw as Dunrannoch's newly arrived lord. The same air of sensual promise. The same dangerous mischief in his eyes.

Sipping from her sweet sherry, Ursula peered at the plaque on the frame: Dougray Dalreagh, thirteenth Earl of Dunrannoch. It had been painted in 1683.

Clan blood clearly ran strong.

"Ah, Miss Abernathy! 'Tis a pleasure to welcome you to the castle. I trust we're making you comfortable." The voice behind her was a little rasping but there was no doubting it as that of Dunrannoch's laird.

Ursula caught her breath. Finlay Dalreagh lacked the strength to hold himself fully upright in his wheeled chair but he bore the same piercing look as the portrait. Even in his weakened state, she recognized the bearing of a man who was accustomed to being master of those around him.

"Forgive me for nae meeting you afore tonight." He fastened his pale eyes upon her—the same grey as Rye Dalreagh's. "Age is both a privilege and a curse." He smiled weakly. "I hadnae thought to see another Yule season, but here we are."

Ursula curtseyed low, managing with scarcely a wobble.

"I must give ye my thanks for taking on my grandson at such short notice." The laird gave a rascallish half-smile. "I've nae doubt he's a handful, being woven from Dunrannoch yarn. Ye have only to look at him to ken that!"

The countess, hovering not far away, kissed her husband's forehead. "No woman minds a handful when it's so handsomely packaged, my love."

Ursula averted her eyes as the earl gave his wife's behind a playful pat. "'Tis your sweet heart that keeps mine young, Lavinia."

"Flirting with all the pretty ones, sir?" The unmistakable Texan drawl of Lord Balmore carried towards them.

"Ha! There's the young scallywag, seeing well to the Dalreagh tartan, too."

The laird spoke nothing but the truth. It was the first time Ursula had seen Rye in much else but his shirtsleeves. Now, he wore a full kilt of dark russet accented with green, and a sporran of beaver, his broad torso encased in an evening jacket, its buttons gleaming.

Though the hair still curled at his neck, his jaw was clean and smooth. Without his stubble, he looked almost a different man, though the glint in his eyes spoke of his wild streak, regardless of the shaving.

Until now, she'd hardly believed Rye might manage what he intended. Not that his accent mattered, nor whether he remembered to butter his bread on his plate. It had simply seemed that he was too much of the outdoors to be polished up and put on display.

As it turned out, he was proving her wrong—and she wasn't quite sure how she felt about it.

THROUGHOUT DINNER, Ursula had ample opportunity to admire Rye further, and to observe the fluttering lashes of Fiona and Bonnie, placed either side. A stream of inanities floated across the table, the girls exclaiming at tales of lassoing steers and cooking rattlesnakes over a campfire.

"Did you really converse with Indian savages?" Lady Bonnie gasped. They seemed surprised that Lord Balmore hadn't been scalped on the spot.

Ursula heard him reply. "The indigenous people prefer to be called by their tribal names." She wanted to listen more but, with the dowager countess on her left and Lady Iona on her right, Ursula was drawn into a conversation on the most effective remedies for chilblains.

They slurped their way through Cullen skink, followed by some rather grey-looking mutton. Ursula pushed it round her plate but it continued to lie apathetic, congealing snugly between two boiled potatoes. Even the clootie dumpling, rich with dried fruit and spices, failed to rouse her appetite.

Rye, meanwhile, asked for a second helping.

At last, the interminable meal was over and the ladies rose.

"They'll only be a few minutes behind us, Bonnie dear." Ursula heard Lady Balmore chivvying her daughter as they entered the drawing room. "Now, don't be afraid to—you know…" She tugged a little at Lady Bonnie's neckline, pulling the yoke to the edge of her shoulders.

"Do you think he's interested, Mama? I can't tell. He seems to look just as much at Fiona as at me, as if he can't decide."

"Of course he likes you." Lady Balmore sniffed. "Now, get

yourself seated at the piano and play something melodious—none of your *doaty* dirges!"

Close behind, the other Lady Balmore—Arabella, wasn't it?—seemed to be taking a different tack with her own daughter. "You're being far too obvious, Fiona. Less smiling if you please. Men like to hunt rather than be chased. In fact, a certain aloofness can work wonders; ignore him all together if you like."

Fiona looked bewildered and wandered over to turn the pages for Bonnie.

With a sigh, Ursula helped herself to the coffee that had been put out on the side.

No sooner had she poured than Lady Balmore was at her elbow. "How thoughtful of you, Miss Abernathy. If you might bring us each a cup that would be most kind." With a curt nod, she lifted the saucer from Ursula's fingers and went to take a seat.

Pursing her lips, Ursula did as she was told.

The laird it seemed, was weary, requiring Lady Dunrannoch to retire with him, leaving Cameron and Rye to join the would-be harem.

"How are ye getting along?" asked Cameron, coming to sit alongside Ursula. "Surviving the vipers' pit?" He chuckled to himself. "I dinnae envy my cousin, being thrown in with these fighting o'er him."

Ursula buried a smile beneath the rim of her cup.

She was more than happy to let Cameron cheer her up a bit. He was a little on the skinny side for her taste, but he might do to make Rye jealous. Despite heading towards her, Lord Balmore had veered away as soon as Cameron sat down, taking an armchair by the fire instead, next to the dowager.

"You're a saint and no mistake, choosing to spend your Hogmany up here in the wilds of Rannoch—in this *dreich* weather, and all for the sake of this *crabbit* lot. They're ne'er happy unless they've something to moan about."

Ursula couldn't help laughing. It was nice to have an ally —even though Cameron was a mite younger than her and didn't seem to hold sway over anyone. Since being introduced, he'd been nothing but friendly.

"They've not been so very *crabbit*—and I don't mind the weather when we're warm inside."

"You're too polite by half, Miss Abernathy. I only hope your good manners rub off on these *tumshie* cousins o' mine."

"*Tumshie?*" Ursula raised an eyebrow.

"Like turnips o'course. Although, to be fair, sometimes, they're more like plain tatties."

"That's a dreadful thing to say!" Ursula laughed again. "On behalf of my gender, I must protest."

"In that case, I shall shut ma blethering and offer ye a wee dram. Grandfather keeps the best locked away in his library, but I know where the key is. I'll be back in two ticks with something to warm ye better than coffee."

No sooner had he departed than Ursula noticed Lady Arabella Balmore staring at her with marked dislike. Ursula fought the urge to poke out her tongue.

Rye was also looking over, and with a wistful expression. No doubt, it was exhausting having a bevy of women tussling over one. She'd overheard his two younger cousins vying to guess his favourite song, only to discover that he'd never heard of any of the ballads they suggested.

He rose from his seat and wandered over, the wolfhound following. It put its head in his lap when he sat down again, gazing up with devoted eyes.

Even the dog is enamoured with him!

Ursula rolled her eyes. "A new friend?"

"You miss your master, don't you, big lug." Rye rubbed behind the wolfhound's ears. "I've been letting Murdo sleep on my bed." He grinned in his usual way. "I don't see why anyone should mind if I don't."

"Well, if it's the best company you can find…" Ursula smiled sweetly and opened up her reticule to extract her pot of salve.

Only too late did she remember.

The little mouse had sat inside cosily all through dinner, so still and quiet that she'd quite forgotten him. Now, he made a leap for the carpet.

With a squeal, Lady Iona jumped onto a chair.

The piano lid crashed—as the tiny varmint skittered up and across the keys.

Murdo began to howl and, from two rooms away, McTavish caught the scent and barrelled in to join the fun.

Both cat and mouse shot at high speed, scampering between petticoats and slippered feet. Cups and saucers went flying and, as Cameron entered the room, so did the whisky. The screaming had reached a fever pitch when Rye made a dive for McTavish.

Ursula, meanwhile, opened her reticule wide and the mouse, sensing its best interests, bounded back in.

Nothing more needed to be said. Ursula whisked from the room, with Rye in pursuit.

"Don't let it out again until I've locked this one away!" Held unceremoniously aloft, McTavish spat and wriggled.

Having witnessed the commotion, the butler had presented himself and, with a nod at the main doors, opened them in readiness. A cold blast of air wafted into the hallway.

"I'm sorry but you're far too much trouble," chided Ursula, whispering into her bag through the cracked clasp. She took three steps outside and gave the mouse its freedom, sending it scuttling through the snow.

It was at that moment that she heard them—bagpipes!

Was someone on the roof?

She craned her head upward. It was impossible to tell, but it sounded as if the music were coming from above.

It was certainly too cold to be standing about outside—either listening or playing.

Darting back into the hall, she near collided with Lord Balmore.

From the open door of the drawing room, the dowager's voice carried out, full-laden with doom. "'Beware! Beware! 'Tis Camdyn, playing on the ramparts."

Staggering to her feet, she outstretched her gnarled finger, pointing into the hall, directly at Rye. "'Tis the Dunrannoch curse, come to claim the next heir!"

CHAPTER FOURTEEN

Mid-morning, 19th December

IT WAS a relief to finally get outdoors. Rye's feet were itchier than a buck's in springtime. He'd never liked being cooped up inside and, these past days, he'd had about as much as he could take.

All those yapping women! They were driving him crazy.

It wasn't just the talk about sashes and gloves and how puffed their darn sleeves ought to be. It was this business about the curse. As far as he could tell, it was a load of balooey. His uncles' deaths had been tragic alright—but the result of some old loon's jinx upon the place?

At worst, someone was playing tricks—for their own amusement, or to see if he was the sort who scared easily. They could suck their teeth 'til they turned blue before he gave them that satisfaction.

Striding across the castle courtyard, he breathed deep, letting the fresh air clear his head.

Besides that nonsense with the curse, there had been Lady Dunrannoch to placate. She'd been discreet in pulling him aside after all the waltzing, but there was no duping her.

The others might have been too caught up in themselves to see him and Ursula spring apart, but Lavinia knew a clinch when she saw one.

Of course, he'd taken the blame onto himself, telling the countess he'd jumped on Miss Abernathy without any sort of provocation. A woman had to guard her reputation and he wouldn't be the cause of Ursula losing hers.

He'd been raised to know the difference between right and wrong and he'd acted reckless. He'd let his pecker do the thinking and near got Miss Abernathy dismissed for it.

The countess had been mighty good about the sorry business—all things considered—but she'd reminded him that Miss Abernathy was there with a job to do. The job of making him decent for 'polite society', as she put it, and that Miss Abernathy was a decent gentlewoman herself.

She'd put him in his place all right, and reminded him that Ursula deserved better than a stand-up grope, delivered where anyone might walk in and see.

There were to be no more private lessons. The countess would sit in herself where she could, or ask one of his aunts to do so.

The upshot was, he'd had not a minute's peace the whole time since.

The only consolation was that Ursula looked as miserable about it as he was. Was it wrong the he hoped she might be hankering after another of those sweet kisses and wondering how they might snatch one?

Doggone it! There he went again.

No matter what his blood was telling him it wanted, he was man enough to know when to leave a woman alone, and there was no excuse for him to forget the promise he'd made.

It included taking on one of those porcelain doll cousins. He just needed to work out which one he'd the best chance of falling for—or which of them seemed most in love with him. A few weeks back, he'd thought it would be pretty simple. A matter of time; nothing more.

Now, a whole heap of reasons kept getting in the way—and they all looked like Miss Ursula Abernathy.

As Rye entered the stable, there was a collective turn of heads from the half doors of each stall. Charon gave a whinny at his approach, bending to breathe into his palm.

"You and me, buddy." Rye rested his forehead against the stallion's nose. "Ready to stretch those legs and take a ride?"

The stable lad, Buckie, appeared beside him and Rye nodded his thanks at the offer of having Charon saddled up. He could do it himself, of course, but that wasn't the point. Everyone employed at the castle had a job to do, and part of Rye's job was to make them feel valued.

Rye took a wander down the stalls, pausing to whisper to each horse.

Only when he came to the last, which was empty, did he hear the muffled sobbing.

"Miss Abernathy?"

She was bundled with a strange assortment of woollens about her neck, and her nose was redder than a pig's pate in the midday heat.

"You all right in there?"

With a self-conscious snuffle, she gathered herself upright and dabbed at her eyes.

Was she hiding out? She didn't exactly look pleased to see him.

"I'm fine. Just…" she sighed heavily. "There are the most delicious smells wafting from the kitchen, and they're putting up the last decorations in the banqueting hall today —for the dance—and raising the Christmas tree. Lady Dunrannoch asked my opinion and I had to tell her the truth."

"Which is?" Rye raised an eyebrow.

"It's the most beautiful thing I've ever seen." Her voice dissolved in a wail.

Rye gave a low whistle. "Well, it sounds awful. No wonder you wanted to get out o' there!"

Ursula gave a choked laugh. "I know it's silly of me. It's only that everyone's so excited, and there's so much bustle, and, and…"

"And you're far from your own folks." Rye finished the sentence for her. "You're thinkin' about the people you'd really like to be with."

She frowned briefly, then nodded. "One person, really." She sniffed. "My father—but he's dead, so I won't ever see him. It's too late!" Ursula dropped her head, giving in once more to tears.

Rye didn't need to think twice. He brought his arm round her.

Sometimes, a person just needed holding.

They stood for a while, until Ursula quietened and wiped her cheeks.

"I have to toughen up. I'm not the only one to have lost a parent." She attempted to laugh. "None of your cousins are out here feeling sorry for themselves."

"I'm out here." Rye leant against the stall's divide.

"I'd forgotten, sorry. I expect you're feeling some of the same things."

"More than likely." Rye gave her his half-smile.

She wasn't alone in losing someone she'd cared about. That was true. But, he'd a feeling there was more than that making her miserable. Whatever relations she did have, she'd decided to be here instead. They must be pretty poor excuses for family if she was choosing his over her own.

Rummaging in her pockets, she drew out a fresh handkerchief.

"No pet mice today?" He gestured at her coat.

She looked bemused, so he nudged a bit further. "No scorpions or snakes?"

Her lips twitched at that. "There aren't any in Scotland—not scorpions anyway."

"That's a relief. Though McTavish could probably handle them."

He rested a hand on her shoulder. "How about I teach you something for a change—just for fun. We can shake out our manes and let the wind blow through."

"You're comparing me to a horse?" Ursula gave her nose a final blow.

"It's the highest compliment." Rye took her hand in his own, leading her out to where Buckie had the stallion saddled. "Know how to canter while standing in the stirrups?"

"You want me to do that? On this enormous beast?" Ursula shook her head, laughing.

"Get good enough an' I'll show you how to stand on the saddle itself. I did it all the time back home." He gave her a wink.

"You may be waiting some time—but don't let me stop you from showing off your talents. I can tell you like an audience."

As if on cue, another voice called across the courtyard. "Off on a jaunt, Balmore? Care if I come along?"

Rye sighed. It was no surprise that Cameron would hunt them out. He'd been showing far too much interest in Miss Abernathy for Rye's liking. Not that she belonged to him; he could hardly claim that, but he didn't know his cousin well enough to guess his intentions.

Despite her bravado, Rye could see Ursula was vulnerable. He wouldn't stand by and watch his cousin lead her down some merry path. He'd come close enough to doing that himself.

"The sun's warmed things up a wee bit, I see." Cameron

rubbed his hands together. "It'll be melting the lighter patches o' snow and giving the coos a proper feed again—but I wanted to check on those grazing east of the bothy. There's a lot of clover in the pasture there and it can give them the bloat if they over-eat."

Rye passed his hand through his hair. "Sounds like we'd best take a scout over there." He cast an apologetic look Ursula's way.

"Here," he passed Cameron the reins. "I'll saddle one of the others. You take Charon and I'll catch up."

"Brodie's stallion?" Cameron blanched. "But—is he safe?"

"Charon? Sure he is!" Rye gave the horse's rump a slap. "I've been ridin' him the whole time. He's solid as a rock."

"Not that I'm feart of the animal, o'course." Cameron gave the horse a doubtful pat.

"Wouldn't think it for a minute." Rye nodded to Buckie, that he might bring round another of the horses. He couldn't help notice the lad was also looking somewhat pale. He'd have a word with Campbell, the head stableman; perhaps Buckie had been working too hard.

With a stiff smile, Cameron brought his boot into the stirrup and swung himself into the saddle.

No sooner had he done so than Charon uttered a full-throated whinny. The stallion reared onto his hind legs, peddling wildly. With a buck, he jumped to the side, throwing Cameron clear out of his seat.

Ursula screamed as the young man flew toward the hard cobbles. His landing came with a horrible thud.

"Dear God!" Rye grabbed at Charon's reins, attempting to calm him before those powerful hooves came down on Cameron's prone body. Something had spooked the beast badly, and even the best of horses were unpredictable when frightened.

The stable lad, meanwhile, was backing away in horror.

"None of that, Buckie!" Rye knew he needed help. "Run for Campbell, quickly."

Ursula was down on her knees already, checking for signs of life.

"He's breathing, and moving his fingers. There's no blood. His head looks fine." She looked up at Rye, her eyes wide with their own terror at what she'd just witnessed.

"What happened?" Cameron raised his chin a little then whimpered in pain.

"You've had a fall." Ursula took Cameron's hand. "Just tell me where it hurts."

Despite her fear, Ursula was doing a marvellous job. Rye felt a surge of pride.

"My shoulder," Cameron gasped. "It's happened once afore. A dislocation. Hurts like the devil."

"We need to get it back in the socket." Rye looked from Cameron to Ursula. "Miss Abernathy, can you follow my instructions?" Though Rye had a firm grip on Charon, the stallion was still skittering. He couldn't afford to let him go, nor trust Ursula to hold him.

"I d-don't know." Ursula looked as if she might be sick.

"Please." Cameron was begging now. "I'm afraid I'll pass out."

"You can do it, Miss Abernathy." Rye kept his voice level. "Take his wrist and bring the arm directly upward, then pull it straight."

Ursula stood, taking Cameron's arm and doing exactly as Rye instructed. Cameron gave a ghastly groan and then a sharp cry before falling quiet again.

Gasping with relief, Ursula buried her head in her hands.

All at once, two different doors opened across the courtyard. From one emerged Campbell, who ran to take Charon from Rye's weary arms. From the other came Lady Balmore; Aunt Arabella few across the cobblestones like a harpy from Hell.

The shriek she gave was most piercing.

"Cameron, my love!" Pushing Ursula out of the way, she fell beside her nephew. "You can't be dead! I won't allow it!"

Rye was dumbstruck. His aunt had never given the impression of caring for anyone in particular. Even her love for her daughter, Fiona, seemed lukewarm.

"How could you?" She turned to Rye with eyes blazing. "You know that horse isn't safe. What were you thinking? It should have been shot after it threw Brodie." Her shoulders heaved in great sobs.

"Your nephew's going to be alright." Ursula ventured toward Lady Balmore. "It could have been much worse."

"Don't touch me!" Lady Balmore smacked away Ursula's hand. "He might have been killed! And it would have been your fault, stupid girl. He would never have attempted getting on that monster if he hadn't been trying to impress you."

Ursula staggered back, her face a horrible shade of grey.

"Now just hold on." There was no way Rye was going to stand by and see Miss Abernathy maligned for something that wasn't her doing. "You're actin' madder'n a steer with a thorn in its side."

"What did you say?" Lady Balmore fell suddenly still.

"You're not thinkin' straight, Arabella. It was an accident, pure and simple."

By now, a small crowd had gathered. Fiona scuttled over to her mother, placing her arms around her shoulders, while Lady Iona came running to her son.

"Let's get everyone inside." The countess made her way through. "If Cameron's had a fall, he'll be in shock. Best to keep him warm. You'll help, Rye? Can you carry him? We'll make him comfortable in the library."

Rye nodded.

An accident, he'd said.

He just wasn't altogether sure he believed it.

CHAPTER FIFTEEN

Later that morning, 19th December

A HALF HOUR passed before Rye came to find her.

"How is he?" She'd been pacing outside the library, not wishing to intrude. Cameron had enough female relatives to fuss over him.

"Just needs to rest up a week or two, and then take it easy. Everything'll heal, as long as he avoids climbing trees."

"Or getting into the saddle of madcap horses." Ursula couldn't help the barb. She'd been replaying the scene over and over—of Cameron taking the reins and hoisting himself upward. Charon had stood nice and steady, just as Rye said he would, right up until the moment Cameron lowered himself onto the stallion's back. Then, all hell had broken loose. Charon had become a different horse entirely.

A muscle ticked in Rye's jaw. "There's nothing wrong with Charon. I'm going out to speak with Campbell. See if I can get to the bottom of this."

"I'll come with you." She had to know. She'd been right there when it happened. Rye had invited her to mount the horse before Cameron had interrupted them. It might have been her…

CAMPBELL WAS RUBBING down Charon with straw, speaking to the horse in the same soothing way Rye always did.

Ursula had to admit that Charon was handsome—finely proportioned and well-muscled, not unlike Rye himself. His eyes, dark and soft and full-lashed, followed Rye as he approached. There was devotion in those eyes, even though Rye had only been riding him these short weeks.

"Stay here." Rye spoke quietly. "Campbell's likely to be more forthcoming if he's just confiding in me."

She accepted with a shrug. It was the same with most things, wasn't it? Women were another species, most of the time—not rational enough in men's eyes, or not to be trusted with hearing unpleasant truths. It was one of the reasons she'd always felt that she didn't want to get married. Men tended to want to put you in a box: housekeeper, mother, wife. They didn't want someone who had ideas of their own, or aspirations.

Not that Rye seemed that way. He appeared to admire the fact she, as Miss Abernathy, was making her own way in the world.

Ursula still wasn't sure exactly what her aspirations were —but something worthwhile beyond looking after a man's home. Her father, clearly, hadn't taken seriously her hopes of running his half of the business. He hadn't believed in her, or not in the way she'd wanted him to.

But she could still believe in herself. She just needed to work out where to direct her energies. She was very fond of dogs, and most animals really. Perhaps she could run a home for them instead of for a husband! A home for animals that other people didn't want, or a home from which they might adopt an animal. She'd give that some thought.

There were only seven more days until she came into the first installment of her inheritance; then, she'd have choices.

Wandering along the stalls, she petted one of the mares. Campbell did a good job with the stable. Every horse looked in good condition—bright eyed and sleek coated.

A few minutes later, Rye joined her, his face drawn. "I've told Campbell to saddle Charon again. I'm taking him out—to prove there's nothing wrong with him."

Ursula's heart gave a lurch. "No!" She looked up into Rye's face, needing him to listen. "It might not be safe...so soon after."

"When Campbell removed the saddle, there was a dried thistle head under the blanket." Rye held her gaze.

"Strange..." Ursula frowned. "But I suppose it must happen round here. There are so many thistles; they grow like weeds."

"They do, but I don't think it's so common that they find their way under saddles." Rye passed his hand over his forehead. "Campbell told me he'd only seen it happen once before. He found the same just after my uncle, the first Lord Balmore, was thrown."

Ursula's hand flew to her mouth. What was Rye saying? That someone had meant his uncle harm? That someone meant him harm as well?

"What about the stable boy?" She remembered how scared the lad had looked. "He was the one who made Charon ready for you. What does he say about it?"

"Buckie's nowhere to be found." Rye rubbed his chin. "It doesn't mean anything, of course. The lad's probably fearful of being dismissed. He'll turn up later, I expect."

"He wouldn't have put the thistle there on purpose, would he?" Ursula worried at her lip. Even as she said it, she knew it was an unlikely theory. What reason would he have to wish harm on anyone in the family. It made no sense.

Rye seemed to agree. None of it made sense. Perhaps the thistle really had gotten under the blanket by accident.

"At least, Lady Balmore can't make you put the horse down, now, can she?" Ursula touched Rye's arm. "Not when she hears what caused the stallion to rear up like that?"

"I doubt she'll think it makes much difference what caused it but, no, I won't let her hurt the horse. It's not the animal's fault. She's just lookin' for someone to blame."

Ursula nodded. She noticed that Rye was wearing a riding coat of tweed today—in shades of grey and moss. It didn't look new, though it fit him reasonably well. Had it been his uncle Brodie's, or been worn by the other one—Lachlan wasn't it? Of course, it made sense for Rye to make use of their serviceable clothing, but something about it made her shiver. It was like stepping into dead men's shoes.

"If you're saddling up, I'll come with you." The declaration was out almost before she'd finished thinking the words. "Just in case." A warmth stole through her cheeks. She was acting impulsively again, she knew, but she had a feeling Rye oughtn't to be alone right now—on the moor, or anywhere else. For all his strength, he needed someone to look out for him.

The frown lines across his forehead eased a little. He brought his palm to her cheek and his lips curled up, giving her his half-smile.

"Sure thing, little bear. I'd be glad of the company."

IT HAD BEEN QUITE a while since Ursula had ridden, not since early in the summer, on the Arrington estate, but the mare was an easy mount, responding to the gentlest of squeezes to her girth.

They set out in the direction Cameron had spoken about. He'd wanted to check on the cattle, so that was what they'd do.

She thought it would give them some good news to report, that the cows were fine. Except that, as they approached, she saw they were anything but fine.

Cameron had been right about the snow melting down here. Wide swathes of grass had been exposed under the sun's warmth. No wonder the cattle had been feasting. They'd have thought all their birthdays had come at once after having to scrape through the snow with their hooves these past days, revealing one small portion at a time.

There were twenty of the great, shaggy cows in all, and they were all lying prone, like balloons with legs sticking out, their stomachs blown up tight. A couple were kicking at their bellies, but most lay still. It looked uncomfortable in the extreme but the cows were making barely any noise.

"They've been gorging alright." Rye jumped down from Charon and helped Ursula do the same. "See how fast they're breathing, with their necks stretched back and their tongues protruding. They must have been like this an hour or two. The bloat isn't just causing their abdomens to swell; it's putting pressure on their lungs."

"Is there anything we can do?" Ursula looked from one cow to the next. Their eyes were bulging but their lowing was faint—an occasional anxious sound, as if they knew what was to come and had already accepted it.

"There might be." Rye leant over the cow nearest them. "I've only done this once before, but the results were immediate." He was feeling between the cow's ribs. "There's a certain place. If you puncture correctly, you can free the gas. It's not ideal, but it's the quickest solution. I don't know what else to try. There's no time to ride for medicine; they'll be dead before we make it back."

"You're going to cut them open?" Ursula felt a wave a nausea rising. "Won't it hurt them?"

"I've no doubt it will, but it's that or leave them to die." From the look on Rye's face, she could see he didn't like the idea either, but he was doing what had to be done.

"We just need something sharp. I usually carry a knife, back home, but I've nothing in these pockets." He thumped at his head. "Damnation. With all that's happened today, I wasn't thinking about what we'd do if we found the cattle in need of help."

Ursula looked again at all the cows. They had to do something. No animal should die in pain. The moor was their home, but its bounty had caused this. The very place that had provided the cows with fodder had turned against them. It was too cruel.

Turning her face to the mountains, she felt the breeze lifting the loose strands of hair from around her face. The sun was warmer than it had been in days. Truly, the moor was beautiful. She wondered how it would look in spring, and in the summer. Did the hillsides turn mauve with blooming heather, as she'd seen in paintings? How much she'd like to see that, to admire the moorland in all its seasons.

The wind tugged at her felt hat and she raised a hand to secure it, her fingers feeling for the pin that held it in place.

The pin!

Of course. It would be sharp enough, wouldn't it?

Swiftly, she removed it, holding it out to Rye, showing him the very thing that might help them.

He took it from her with a grin.

"Looks like you just saved them, little bear."

By the time Rye was done, they'd gotten every cow back on

its feet. Mostly, the cattle looked disoriented, staggering slightly, clustering together, giving their neighbours friendly licks.

Had they known how close they'd come to death? Such animals were thought to be stupid, but Ursula wasn't so sure. Several of them nudged Rye with their noses, as if giving thanks for the relief he'd brought them.

Finally, the two of them drove the cattle away from where the clover had been exposed, kicking snow back over where they could.

"You did it!" Ursula beamed at him. It had been a marvellous thing to watch—Rye at work, doing something she'd never dreamed possible. Dunrannoch had struck lucky the day Rye Dalreagh came back to claim his title.

"We did it." Rye wrapped his arm about her shoulders. "You were braver than many a man I've seen, helping get these ladies upright. I couldn't have done it without you."

She knew it wasn't true. He'd done all the work. She'd pushed alongside him, but it had been his strength that had helped the cows gain their legs again.

The sun was already dipping but she didn't want to go back to all the bustle and commotion that had nothing to do with her—to the family life from which she was excluded.

She wanted to stay with Rye. Just he and her. They were a good team. She'd been forcing him to learn a whole lot of nonsense these past days—things he mostly would never need to know, things she'd dredged up from her time at Monsieur Ventissori's Academy. Rye had never once complained. He'd knuckled down because he thought it was the right thing to do.

She might have been teaching him, but there was a whole lot she was learning—and not just about cows.

"What now?" She willed him to look into her eyes and see what she was really thinking.

He pulled her into his chest and touched his lips to her

forehead, then down the plane of her nose. She tipped her head back to invite his mouth upon hers. As his kiss truly found her, she let go, opening to every tug and sip, and the gentle intrusion of his tongue.

His arms came gradually tighter, until he was lifting her, resting her behind in the crook of his arms, so that it was she, now, who looked down at him. The advantage of height let her take control of the kiss, and she delighted in it, weaving her fingers through his hair, pulling back his head so that she might look him full in the face. She tasted him everywhere, brushing her lips to his eyebrows and eyelids— to his lashes even. To the course stubble regrowing on his jaw, and his mouth. She was falling into him, wanting to be held like this forever.

A kiss like that should never end, but she knew there was more. The way he was holding her—his arms so strong, lifting her up—was making her heart beat fast, heating her up inside, and she had the strangest feeling; a desire to wrap her legs around his waist and push herself against him.

She'd never read of such a thing. Had never thought of it before. But her body was telling her what it wanted.

Rye.

CHAPTER SIXTEEN

Late afternoon, 19th December

THERE HAD BEEN a chapter in that book of Miss Abernathy's, about seizing opportunities and not wasting the life you had. If there was something she wanted, she had to take it, or risk never knowing what might have been.

As she led Rye towards the bothy, she knew what she was doing—as much as it was possible to know. She'd never been with a man before; of course, she hadn't. But she knew she wanted more than Rye's kiss.

She wanted to feel his skin again. She wanted to drag off his shirt and run her hands over his back. She wanted to kiss not just his mouth but his neck and shoulders, and his chest. She wanted to feel the hardness and softness of him all at once, and she wanted his hands on her that way too.

She'd run away to where no-one would find her, and where no-one knew who she was. She'd told herself it was an adventure, in which she got to play at being someone else, and didn't need anyone's approval, except that she wasn't being someone else now. She was being herself.

And she wanted to know what it would feel like to be utterly herself with Rye.

She wasn't hurting anyone. He wasn't engaged yet. He hadn't chosen, although he was going to. Whatever happened here, it had nothing to do with the choices he'd make later.

She wasn't asking him for love. Wasn't asking him for anything but this moment between them. This would be hers. Her decision. Because she could.

Inside, the bothy was just as they'd left it.

He worked quickly to get the woodburner lit, throwing on all the kindling in one go and then heaping up the peat.

She'd already removed her jacket and her skirt, and her fingers trembled over the buttons of her shirtwaist.

Still kneeling by the stove, he looked up, watching her. "You don't have to…"

But she carried on, drawing down the sleeves of the blouse and casting it off, until she was standing in her combination and corset.

"I want you to kiss me again, Rye, and then everything else a man does with a woman."

"Everything?" He looked taken aback.

"I'm not a strumpet—or not until now. I've never done this before." Somehow, it seemed important to say it; for the sake of honesty—although he probably knew already. How could he not?

"I could never think badly of you." He stood up.

"In that case, help me." She turned, showing him the laces. They weren't tight—only pulled as far as she'd been able to manage on her own that morning.

He tugged, loosening them far enough that she could step out.

With her back to him, she paused. His hand was resting on her hip, warm fingers on soft cotton.

"You're sure," he said again.

"I don't want half. I want all of it. I trust you, and I want you to show me."

She was very much aware of him standing behind her—of his breath on the bare skin of her shoulder, where the yoke of her chemise had slipped to one side.

"It's something special, little bear." He brought his fingers to her collarbone, touching very lightly.

"That's why I want it to be you."

"Even though…" His voice trailed off. He knew, she supposed, that he didn't need to say it; not for her benefit. They both knew.

He wasn't going to be hers.

She wasn't going to be his.

Whatever happened, it was just for this moment in time.

And that was fine—because it was her choice. No matter what happened, she'd always have this. It would be her secret, tucked safely from the judgement of others.

She turned around and gave him a smile. "You need to catch up. I'm not taking off the rest until you've shown me everything."

"Yes, ma'am." With top coat and boots gone, he peeled off his shirt and tossed it to one side.

His chest was just as broad and muscled as she'd known it would be—like the statues in the British Museum, but far from marble cold. His skin was a light brown, marked at the shoulders by the sun. And there was hair on his chest—curling thick like the mane on his head, covering all the way to a dark arrow pointing downward, disappearing within the waistband of his trousers.

Her eyes were fixed there, on that trailing line. She had an inkling where it led to. Not all statues wore fig leaves, after all. And she'd felt the outline of what he kept in his trousers, too—the first time he'd kissed her, and again, outside; something hard that wanted to poke at her belly.

"Keep going."

She wanted to see it.

He tipped his fingers in mock salute and slowly pulled through his belt. She watched him unbutton the fly, letting the trousers drop. With only his small garments beneath, the outline of his manhood was apparent. It pushed out against the fabric, making a tent in front.

"These as well?" He was teasing, pulling out the waistband and peeking inside. "Are you sure your maidenly sensibilities can cope?"

"Uh huh." She licked her lips. There was no doubt in her mind.

And then, they were off.

He stood entirely naked, backlit by the fire. The front of his body was half-shadowed but she saw enough to know that he was a prime specimen of man.

The hair sprung thick between his legs, but it did nothing to hide that part of him a man used for reproduction.

She felt hot and lewd, wanting to touch him—was struck by a yearning to rub her cheek over him; not just over the fur of his chest and that flat abdomen but along his thighs and…

Her heart was racing.

Had she really just thought that?

Yes. She wanted to rub her face over his penis.

Not just her face.

She wanted to open her mouth and taste it.

What was wrong with her?

She was depraved, surely.

Except that, looking at Rye, and seeing how he was looking at her, it didn't feel like it could be wrong.

Keeping her eyes on this new part of him, she pulled the ribbon of her chemise and shimmied it downward, then did the same with the ribbon on her drawers.

Suddenly, she was as naked as he, feeling a little goosebumped and uncertain.

Was her body as much a surprise to him? It wasn't the

first he'd seen, she expected, but women came in different shapes. What would he think of her, now that she was showing him everything?

Before she had a chance to ask, he stepped closer and answered whatever she was thinking with his hands. Warm and firm, they moved over her breasts, cupping their weight. His thumb and forefinger grazed her nipples.

"Rye." She breathed his name rather than spoke it, and he bent his head to her neck, kissing down to her shoulder and then up again, into her nape and hair.

His kisses, first tender, grew fervent—his mouth and lips and tongue eating her up and all the while murmuring endearments, telling her she was perfect, and that he couldn't stop touching her, that he wanted to taste and squeeze and own every part.

He kissed her mouth again, long and hard, while his hands stroked the arch of her spine and the dimples above the curve of her bottom, and then he brought his lips to the top of her breasts, kissing their softness.

He covered every part of them with his mouth, drawing the peak of her nipple deep inside, then letting it free, gazing upon the bud a moment before pulling it back into the warmth for a second feasting, suckling like a babe hungry for nourishment.

Moving lower, he grazed his stubble over her belly, telling her what he wanted to do—that he was going to kiss her there and make her wet for him.

And then, he was actually doing it, without waiting for her to say no or yes.

Not that she wanted to say no—not to any of it.

He'd fallen to his knees and was breathing through her tangle of curls, his hands reaching round to caress her behind.

She pushed at his head, giggling. There was nothing there

for him to kiss. It was silly. She didn't know what he was doing.

But then he pulled her knee onto his shoulder and brought his mouth straight between her legs, and his tongue was on her cleft.

"Rye!" she gasped, wriggling. "What are you—?"

And then she knew, for his nose was buried in her curls and his tongue was pushing inside her, and it was the most terrible, wonderful thing.

With his hands firm on her behind, he was pulling her onto his face, wanting to do this to her as much as she was enjoying having him do it. She pushed her hips forward and he moaned.

"So beautiful." He was muttering again and holding her tight, drawing the flat of his tongue across that secret part of her and then tickling her with the tip, making her writhe with exquisite, sharp-sweet pleasure.

Right there, where he was teasing her, she was growing hot and restless, melting onto his tongue. He kept pressing and circling, and clasping her in such a way that she couldn't hope to escape from the deep, sweet ache.

Without realising it, she'd wrapped her fingers in his hair and was pushing herself just as hard, panting "No" and then "Yes", and "Oh" and "Yes" again. Something burning bright was coming for her and she didn't know how to stop it. It was bowling her over and tossing her and making her push harder against him.

She didn't know what sounds she was making, only that she couldn't prevent them. His tongue was drawing them out of her, and she was shaking and trembling. And then the burning consumed her utterly and made her cry and tug his hair so hard she must have hurt him, but he only held her tighter.

"Ursula." Her name was rough on his lips. He looked up at her with eyes half-closed but entirely focused.

"I need to be inside you now. That part of myself that's hard, it's all for you. I need to bury myself inside you. It's how a man gives a woman a child, but I won't let that happen. I can stop before that happens."

He was already rising, cupping his arm under her knees and carrying her.

The blanket was still on the bed from the first time.

Gently, he laid her down and kneeled above her.

She couldn't stop looking at that part of him. Where it had bobbed half-upright before, it looked different now: thicker, longer, and wet at the tip.

In the same way that he'd made her wet, she'd done this to him.

By God, she was lovely.

She'd stripped everything away—not just her clothing but her soul, and he was so hard for her, he didn't know where to begin. She deserved to be worshipped.

Not just screwed—which was what the prostitutes in San Antonio had given him. He'd only been a handful of times, and it had all been over pretty quickly. The women he'd lain with had seemed perfectly happy with that—a customer who paid his coin and did what he'd come to do. It had been nothing like this.

He knew what it felt like to enter a woman's body; knew what sorts of noises a woman made when she was liking it, too. But, Ursula was a virgin. Everything that happened between them would be the first time for her.

He'd have to be careful not to hurt her—and to watch himself, too. It was going to be damn difficult, but he couldn't spill inside her. He'd protect her from that, however much his body was telling him otherwise.

He wanted to lick and bite and taste her all the way down

and up again, to bury himself balls-deep and pulse his desire into the velvet heart of her—but this wasn't about him. It was about him showing her what she meant to him.

He'd filled his hands with her, making her pant and mewl as he squeezed and tugged—but not too hard.

He couldn't be too rough with her, but he'd been just rough enough. He wanted her to know that he was taking charge; taking charge of her body and her pleasure. She'd asked him to show her what this was about, and he didn't plan to disappoint.

He hadn't been sure if she'd let him kiss between her legs but she'd taken to it without too much embarrassment. Better than that. He knew where a woman's most intense sensations were and he'd found that place for Ursula. Hearing her moan had been headily arousing. The smell of her, and the beauty of her body, the heat of what she was offering him—all of it was arousing, but most especially the trust she was investing in him.

When she'd come in his mouth, he'd almost spent on the floor, right underneath her.

Now, he moved his weight over her, pushing forward with his hips until the shaft of his erection lay against her cleft.

He groaned into the hollow of her throat.

"I'm ready, Rye. I want you. Don't worry about it hurting. I know it will—but it will be all right. My body's made for this, isn't it—it's made for you."

Hearing her say it tipped him over the edge.

He shifted the angle of his pelvis and his cock, swollen with desire he could barely contain, and found the soft wetness she'd created for him. He drew the broad crown down her cleft, then pushed just the tip inside, rubbing against the swollen part of her. She looked up at him with wide eyes and parted lips.

She trusts you.

He had to remind himself. This wasn't about him; it was for her.

"I don't want to hurt you." No, he didn't—but the ache in his balls was going to rupture him unless he did what he needed to do.

He couldn't hold off any longer.

He wanted to drive his cock into her heat.

He want to thrust home and ride her senseless.

He pushed forward.

Mine.

He sank deeper.

This is mine.

She tensed and gasped—but he was inside her, where it was tight and hot, and soft and—nothing had ever felt so good.

IT HAD HURT. She'd known it would; a sharp burning as he'd entered her.

But it wasn't hurting any more. There was too much slipperiness for that.

He was sliding into her, moving in a steady rhythm and, despite the chill of the room, she was burning hot.

He was, too. There was perspiration on his skin, making his chest stick to hers, dragging rough against her breasts.

The way he was rubbing against her was exciting, making something build again. Something raw. Something she needed. She was on the edge of it and it was different to what he'd done with his tongue.

That had been tender. Reverential even.

This was utterly carnal.

He was moving quickly, pumping fast, then faster. What had begun slowly sped and tumbled, as if they were racing to some invisible finish line.

She tipped back her head to let him see her and wrapped her legs around his, tipping her hips where he was joined to her. She was aware, suddenly, of all the places in which their bodies were touching. That thought, alone, excited her. That there was nothing between them. He was inside her and she wanted him there.

The heat was growing, as if it would ignite her in a great flash, licking through her belly and thighs and sparking right at the spot where they were joined; a huge, blinding flame of pleasure covering every part of her but centred right there, in the place that was giving him pleasure too.

She dragged her nails over his shoulders, needing him to do just this. If he stopped, she would scream, but her voice already seemed to be doing that. A wave of uncontrollable joy swept through her and she arched into him again.

Suddenly, he was groaning and looking down with a surprised expression, as if he didn't quite believe she was there with him.

"Dear God! Ursula!"

HE THRUST one last time and went still, his face buried in her hair.

His body was humming for her—utterly spent, but fiercely alive too.

What had passed between them had been incredible.

Only one thing was wrong. Deep inside, he'd given her every drop of his release.

He should have been horrified. And, yet, part of him was glad.

How hadn't he seen it before?

He wasn't just attracted to Ursula. He was in love. And telling himself anything else was just plain dishonest.

He'd been so busy thinking what he needed to do to make

other people happy, he'd forgotten that he deserved happiness himself. And Miss Ursula Abernathy did more than make him happy. She made his heart sing.

She acted fearless—even when he knew she was shaking with fear, and she was thoughtful—even when nobody else seemed to give her a second thought.

He ought to get down on one knee here and now and beg her to marry him. Nothing else mattered, did it, in the end? He could still do his duty without marrying one of his cousins. He'd make it his duty to find them each a better husband than he could have been.

But, if he was going to propose, he needed to do it right—not on this tatty mattress in a shepherd's bothy, without even a ring to offer her.

He'd get her safely back to the castle and then arrange a meeting with his grandfather. It wouldn't be an easy conversation, but nothing worth having ever came easy.

It was time he stood up for what he knew was right for him—and he wouldn't make his proposal until he'd convinced his family to accept his choice of bride.

If his future truly was here, at Dunrannoch, he wanted Miss Ursula Abernathy to share that future with him. Nothing, and no-one, was going to stand in the way.

CHAPTER SEVENTEEN

Early-evening, 20th December

Ursula sat before the fire in her room, brushing out her hair.

She'd known that nothing would be the same afterward. She'd been a virgin and now she wasn't, but it wasn't just her body that had changed. In those moments afterwards, stroking Rye's back, she'd felt an overpowering tenderness.

He'd leaned up on one elbow and looked at her, and what she'd seen had thrilled her.

Because something in him was different, too.

They were both alive and joyous and vibrant, and what they'd shared was like nothing else in the world.

Was it so wrong of her, now, to harbour a secret hope—that what had happened had deeper meaning for them both?

Throughout the day, guests had been arriving for the countess' Yuletide cèilidh and there seemed no-one in the house unaffected by the excitement.

The banqueting hall was dazzling—every surface flickering with candles and a hundred baubles in gold and silver between, their facets catching the glinting light. The

Christmas tree was swathed in ribbons and all manner of sweet confectionaries, and boughs of green swung from the rafters.

There was a magical atmosphere within the castle, but Ursula felt a pang at what this night might bring.

Lady Dunrannoch had said she would encourage Rye to select from amongst his cousins. Would there be an announcement then, before all the guests?

Though Cameron would be unable to dance, he was recovered enough to attend and had refused to allow any adjustment to the plans on his account. He would sit with his grandfather, he said, and enjoy the festivities from a comfortable chair.

Ursula had hoped that Rye would seek her out, but he'd been closeted with the earl most of the day—discussing his various duties, she supposed.

Or which of his cousins he'll be marrying…

Ursula laid out her blue silk with the smallest of sighs, and was about to change into it when there was a knock upon her door.

"Lady Iona?" Ursula stepped back to allow the earl's daughter entry. "Is everything all right?"

"You won't mind my intrusion, I hope." Iona glanced about the room's meagre furnishings. "I wanted to thank you for helping Cameron. With so much commotion yesterday, I fear your kind efforts were overlooked."

"I did nothing at all," Ursula protested. "The level-head was all Lord Balmore's. I acted only as he instructed."

"Nevertheless, I'm indebted." Lady Iona pressed her hand upon Ursula's. "And I've brought something." Over her arm, she was carrying a length of amber-golden tulle. "The warm tones should suit your complexion. It was a favourite of mine in the year my husband courted me." The colour rose to Lady Iona's cheeks. "We shall not recall how many years ago that was, suffice to say that I had Cameron the following year, and the dress never fitted again. I should long ago have passed the gown to someone who would gain pleasure from wearing it." She laid it carefully beside Ursula's upon the bed.

Beneath the tulle was a layer of palest peach silk, while golden threads embroidered the yoke of the bodice. It was not in the current fashion, but the elegance of the gown was timeless.

A surge of gratitude filled Ursula's chest. "It's truly beautiful, and I'll be honoured to wear it."

The thoughtfulness of the gift touched her more deeply than she could say. She'd seen herself only as an outsider at the castle, but this kind action spoke otherwise.

"I trust you'll enjoy this evening, Miss Abernathy, though we may be a little topsy-turvy, due to Lord Balmore's novel suggestion."

Intrigued, Ursula invited Lady Iona to take the armchair by her fire.

"Food and beverages are to be set out along one side for guests to help themselves," explained Lady Iona, "So that our staff can join in the dancing—at least for an hour or two."

How like him, thought Ursula. She added another brick of peat to the fire and stirred the embers.

Lady Iona seemed in no hurry to leave. There was something wistful in her manner, and perhaps rather sad. Even in a house so filled with people, one might be lonely, Ursula knew.

For some moments they sat in companionable silence, until Iona spoke again.

"The Yuletide cèilidh used to be such a gay affair, but it's harder to persuade guests to make the journey these days, even with the train coming across the moor." She gave a deep sigh. "Of course, we cancelled altogether last year, and Lady Dunrannoch was adamant that, since it's only been just over a year since Lachlan's passing, we should invite only a handful of the local notables and their families. Now, at least, with the whole household invited, we're sure to see some jollity. Lord Balmore is insistent that everyone should enter into the Christmas spirit."

"And I'm sure they shall." Ursula nodded her encouragement.

"Arabella—the first Lady Balmore I should say—is terribly put out," Iona went on. "But I think it's a wonderful idea. It's been far too long since we organized something of this sort—for all the household to enjoy. The Countess was a little taken aback but she's come round quickly—with the proviso that staff will need to return to their duties at ten o'clock."

Ursula suppressed a smile.

"Arabella's a good sort really but she's never understood Highland life. She's from an old Stirling family and wants to make us just as grand here. She doesn't seem to appreciate that the Dalreagh clan are moorland people. We've a brave history of raising arms and doing battle but, these days, we're little more than farmers. The way Arabella carries on, you'd think we should be having royalty to dine every other week! Truly, I think she'd be happiest setting up home again in the city. I've made the suggestion more than once, but she seems remarkably attached to the idea of remaining here. I suppose we can't always understand people's motives."

"It sounds as if the new Lord Balmore has the right idea, anyway." Ursula's heart warmed, hearing all that Iona had to say of him.

"Yes, and he and Cameron have been getting along splendidly. Lord Balmore has proven himself to be very much 'hands on', wanting to learn everything—and seeking out Cameron's advice."

"That's good to hear. And—" Ursula hesitated, uncertain if Iona would think her speaking out of turn, "Cameron doesn't feel resentful of Lord Balmore having swooped in, as it were, and claimed what might have been his?"

Lady Iona shook her head. "Quite the reverse. You see, it's always been Cameron's wish to practise veterinary medicine. He began at the university a few years ago but felt obliged to return to Dunrannoch once Brodie and Lachlan were gone. Grandfather wasn't well enough to manage alone and we needed a male member of the family to take charge. The arrival of Lord Balmore has him 'off the hook' as it were— although I know he'll be pleased to continue giving whatever support he can. He's only twenty-two but he's grown up here and there's very little he doesn't know."

"And, I hope you won't think me forward in asking, but how does the other Lady Balmore feel about things? She's still grieving I know, but does she wish to continue making her home here?"

"Oh, Mary?" Lady Iona looked thoughtful. "Her own family are from Aberdeen—something big in fishing. I don't think she's terribly happy here, but nor does she seem keen on going back to the coast. I suppose she might remarry, in time, but really, it's her girls she cares about most." Iona frowned. "If we're to find husbands for them all, it would make sense for her to take them to town. Lachlan didn't leave her a great deal of personal wealth, but she has a set of rooms in a townhouse in Edinburgh. If grandfather might settle something on her, I believe she'd be delighted."

Lady Iona gave an embarrassed laugh. "I'm sorry. I babble on sometimes. Please forgive me. Our family trials are our own affair—and nothing for you to worry over, Miss Abernathy. I'm sure you have your own future to look to, and will be glad to leave behind this rather desolate place."

"I'm happy to lend a listening ear." Ursula touched the other woman's arm. "And I'll never forget Dunrannoch, nor the moor. I won't regret the time I've spent here."

Lady Iona rose at last. "I must get ready, and leave you to do the same." She gave Ursula a warm smile. "Come and find me amidst the crowd, Miss Abernathy."

As the hour chimed seven, Ursula put the finishing touches to her appearance and clicked shut her door behind her.

No matter what transpires, I must remember that I'm my own woman. Just six more days and I won't need to rely on anyone for shelter or support. I may easily live quietly.

The thought should have been gratifying but, strangely, it was not. She'd never cared for Society, but Lady Iona's visit had reminded her of the comfort of friendly companionship. As for love, with the man she'd come to feel so much for, Ursula hardly dared hope.

Lord Balmore's heart was unknown to her, but he'd spoken so much of duty. How could she fit into his plans? Even were she to reveal her true family connections, and the wealth that was soon to come to her, she was not a Dalreagh. The Earl and Countess Dunrannoch had made things clear; they wanted Rye's bride to come from within their own circle.

She believed she could make Rye happy—perhaps even find contentment in helping him run Dunrannoch—but she couldn't expect him to break with his family for her sake.

She'd just turned the first spiral on the old stone stairs and was deep in her musings when she was brought up sharply by voices just below, rising from the third-floor corridor. Only Rye and Cameron occupied rooms here, Ursula understood, and both should have been downstairs by now—but the abrupt whispers were those of a man and woman, clearly engaged in an argument of sorts.

"Can't carry on like this…has been a mistake." The man's hushed tone was insistent.

"Is there someone else? After all I've been to you…"

"Of course not, but—"

There was a pause, in which Ursula would have sworn the two were kissing.

Could she continue downward? To eavesdrop made her uncomfortable, but she feared the couple might hear her footfall and realize she'd been listening.

The woman's voice had turned sultry. "Come to my bed again tonight…it's only you I think of."

"Impossible. You don't know what you're saying." The man's voice again. "Arabella—this has gone on long enough."

Ursula felt her legs tremble.

Arabella? Lady Balmore?

And the man's voice. Was that Cameron?

Was such a thing possible?

The two weren't related by blood, but relations between them would be unseemly. And how long had they been together? Lady Balmore's husband had been dead nearly two years, but to begin an affair of this sort?

Ursula shook herself.

What was she thinking? She'd never styled herself a hypocrite, nor wished to judge others. If Cameron and his uncle's widow were in love, it wasn't for her to criticise.

And it was wrong of her to linger. She'd heard more than she should already.

Gathering her skirts, she placed one slippered foot before the other, taking the steps as quietly as she could. She would cup the flame of her candle as she passed the opening of the stairs onto the corridor and hope they were too engrossed to notice her passing.

Setting her eyes to watch only the treads before her, Ursula resumed her descent. It had grown quiet, as if the two lovers were again embracing. All the better, for they were unlikely to sense her passing.

She'd almost reached the second floor and begun to breathe more easily when a spider's web loomed in front of her and Ursula stumbled. The candlestick flew from her grasp, clattering down several steps before rolling to a stop. With a gasp, she pressed her back to the wall.

"Did you hear that?" Lady Balmore's voice floated downward. "Someone's there."

Ursula remained frozen. They wouldn't come down the stairs after her, would they?

"One of the maids. That's all. Everyone else is downstairs —and I'm joining them." Cameron sounded exasperated.

"This isn't over. We aren't over!" Lady Balmore's voice hissed. "You'll thank me in the end Cameron, when you realize my true devotion. No one will love you as I do."

"I'm not listening to any more. Now Rye's here, there's no reason for me to remain. The sooner I get away, the better— for you as well, Arabella."

"No!" Her voice rose but Cameron's footsteps were already fading in the opposite direction.

Ursula let out a long exhalation.

Poor Lady Balmore. However unwise the liaison, she felt for her.

As Ursula continued downward, Lady Balmore went to the staircase and peered through the gloom. With silent footsteps she followed, but the figure ahead of her scurried too quickly for her to see properly who had been listening.

She caught only a glimpse of the woman's hem.

No servant but someone in a golden-hued gown, the fabric fine.

CHAPTER EIGHTEEN

A little later...

THE PARTY WAS WELL-UNDERWAY.

Lady Iona had been right. The staff appeared delighted to have been invited to the early part of the evening. Wearing their Sunday best, maids and footmen were whirling to the strains of an Eightsome Reel, to the accompaniment of a small band of players placed in the minstrel's gallery.

The countess and Earl Dunrannoch looked on, with the dowager sitting to her son's right, and Lady Iona and Cameron alongside, joined by some of the older guests.

Lady Iona smiled and nodded, clearly pleased that Ursula was wearing the dress. She'd been right that it suited her. The fit was almost exact and the colours within the gown paired well with the warm tones of Ursula's hair, which she'd pinned up with a golden ribbon threaded through the curls.

She'd find some moment to speak to Rye later, she expected, and it would be something to stand before him looking her best. Her vanity required that, at least.

Ursula stole a longer glance at Cameron.

He looked far from happy.

Little wonder, thought Ursula, knowing what she did.

Broken love affairs could hardly be pleasant things—and Lady Balmore hadn't taken Cameron's rejection well.

She looked out at the dancers. Among the throng, kicking up their heels, were the five young ladies from whom Rye was expected to choose his bride. As laughing people whirled by, Ursula caught a glimpse of Lord Balmore. Standing a head taller than anyone else, he couldn't remain hidden long.

Perhaps there wasn't much difference between her and Arabella. She'd given herself to Rye without expectation of anything further between them, yet she hoped that Rye would remember her as more than a fling.

She ought to join in the dancing at the next opportunity but, for now, she would watch. Mrs. Middymuckle had done a marvellous job with the refreshments, which were laid out along one end of the room. Fruit jellies and blancmanges and dainty tartlets wobbled alongside great plates of cold meats and cheeses. There was a huge punchbowl from which guests could serve themselves, and several bottles of champagne sat in a trough of ice.

Only Mrs. Douglas, the housekeeper, seemed disapproving, standing beside the beverages and glaring at any of her staff who dared take more than a small cupful of the punch.

Ursula hadn't attended an event like this since her season, which had only ended with her persuading her father not to bother with any more such extravagance. She'd declared that she'd find a husband in good time, rather than through an endless round of asinine parties, and he'd never pushed her to fulfil that vow. But wasn't this what her own life was supposed to be like? Dances and parties and having fun? And dreaming of someone special to be in love with?

Her season hadn't made her happy. And she'd certainly not found anyone she wanted to spend her life with. All she'd been able to think of was wanting to work alongside her father. It was him she'd wanted to be close to, and no other man was a worthy comparison.

He'd known, she hoped, how happy she was to stay with him—that no suitor had lived up to her idea of what a man should be.

It had never occurred to her that he'd die.

Nor that he'd fail to secure the passing of his half of the business to Ursula.

And, now, here she was, among people she'd never met, pretending to be someone else altogether.

It was almost fitting, for she barely knew who she was anymore, nor what she wanted. She kept telling herself that she could take care of herself and, of course, she knew that she could—but it didn't mean that it was all she wanted.

A couple of male guests drifted over, surveying the cold buffet with interest.

"He's nae bad looking, I suppose, for an American," one was saying. "Not that it matters, o'course. Those girls would take him whether he was young and sprightly, or hunch-backed and with n'er a tooth in his head."

The other laughed. "I'm sure they're making themselves amenable. There's few would turn down the chance to be countess—and it will nae be long afore Dunrannoch passes on the mantle."

"True enough. And a man disnae need to be in love to marry. Hot and willing is all we ask when it comes to bedding."

As they chuckled, Ursula fought down welling nausea.

Hot and willing.

She'd been that all right.

And Rye certainly hadn't said no.

She'd made it easy for him; and had thought it was easy for her, as well. She'd never imagined how far her feelings would become involved. No matter how she tried to fool herself, she couldn't get away from the truth of it.

Somehow, her heart had become tangled up.

Rye had won her admiration and her respect, and she'd given herself to him without any consideration for what he might truly feel for her.

Since their return from the bothy, she'd been waiting—believing he would seek her out, but he'd been too busy to make time for her.

Actions spoke louder than words, didn't they, and whatever he did feel for her, it wasn't enough to divert him from the path his family had laid out for him.

Would he be different if he knew she was an heiress? If he knew her grandfather had been a viscount?

She was glad he didn't know. Clearly, she wasn't good enough just as she was.

THE MUSICIANS DREW the reel to a close and there was much applause from the floor. Anticipating a small break, most of the dancers were moving towards the refreshments, crowding around Ursula.

It was too much.

She couldn't breathe.

Ursula made her way to the edge, by the window, looking for the best route of escape. Bounded by unfamiliar faces, she was aware again that she didn't belong there.

She'd made up her mind.

In the morning, she'd ask which of the guests might be travelling towards Fort William and join them in leaving the castle. She'd make her way to Daphne. Suddenly, she wanted nothing more than to see her old friend again.

With a sob, she pushed forward, blindly—not seeing anything anymore, or anyone.

"Whoa there!" A firm hand landed on her elbow, dragging her back. "I've been lookin' everywhere for you, little bear."

She knew, straightaway, it was Rye, but it was too humiliating to play this game, and she didn't want him to see she was crying.

"Ursula, what's wrong?" His voice softened, his face creasing in confusion. "You're upset. Has some fella been hasslin' you?" His eyes travelled over her. "You're sure lookin' beautiful tonight, but it's no excuse for a man to foist unwanted attentions."

She was too weary to explain what she was upset about. And what was the use, since it wouldn't change anything.

"I wanted to speak with you," she said at last, "but I know you've been busy. It doesn't matter." She turned away.

"Hold on a minute, Ursula. I've been busy, it's true— mostly talkin' with my grandfather. I've had a few things to set straight, and I couldn't come find you until I'd made sure he understood."

"Discussing your choice of bride." There was a flatness in her voice—a misery she couldn't put into words.

"Yes—but, how did you know?" Rye grinned. "It don't matter. All that does is that I've made him see who it is I should be marryin'. He was a mite surprised but he says he won't make the same mistake he did with my father. His disapproval only drove a wedge between them. Old Finlay doesn't want to repeat that estrangement. As long as I'm happy, he says he is too."

Ursula was too distressed to follow all he was saying, but if he'd chosen baby-faced Blair above her older siblings, Ursula didn't want to know about it. Had he no sensitive feeling?

Clearly not, because he was taking both her hands in his, not caring who might see them.

"Ursula, it's you I want, and I'm hoping you'll say yes." From his pocket, he extracted a ring. "This was my mother's, and I know she'd be pleased to see you wearing it." He lowered his voice a little, glancing about. "I got carried away, yesterday, when we were alone in the bothy. I made a mistake, but no matter what happens, we can put it right. It don't matter to me where you're from or what your family are and, if there's a baby, it'll be born in wedlock. I won't let you face anything alone, little bear."

Ursula frowned, looking at the ring and then at Rye.

"If there's a baby?" She wasn't sure what he meant.

"It was all my fault. You must've noticed? I didn't…" His brow creased in embarrassment. "I didn't do what I should've to protect you from that. It was just so doggone amazing, I lost my head."

He held the ring in front of her finger. "You were wonderful, Ursula. You *are* wonderful. Just say 'yes' and I'll slip this on right away. There's no need for us to wait. You know how it works here? All we need do is declare ourselves married before witnesses and it's good as done. They don't mess about up here. O'course, we can have a formal ceremony later, with a white dress and all the fancies, but we don't need to wait a moment longer. Just say it, Ursula. Say "yes" and be my bride, right here and now."

Ursula felt her legs buckle under her. He wanted to marry her because he got carried away and made a mistake? Because he thought she might be pregnant? Did that happen when you'd only had a man inside you once? She supposed it could. It hadn't occurred to her that it was a likelihood. Rye had murmured something about taking care of that side of things and she hadn't given it another thought.

But she understood now.

He was asking her to marry him because he felt he should —that it was the "right" thing to do. Not because he loved her, or couldn't live without her. Not because he needed her and couldn't bear to let her go. Only because he had a sense of honour, and he thought she might be carrying the next Dunrannoch heir.

It would be easy to say yes—to let him slip that ring on

her finger, but was that what she wanted? Didn't she deserve better? If she was to give up on her plan for independence and entrust her future to a man, she needed to know he wanted her for the right reasons.

Slowly, she curled her fingers into her palm.

"Ursula?" Rye's voice wavered. "Am I takin' things too fast? I can give you more time if you need it."

With her stomach turning somersaults, Ursula made herself look into his eyes. It was breaking her heart to do this —to turn down what she would have grasped with her whole heart, if only he'd asked her in a different way, if only she believed he was asking her for the right reasons.

"Rye...I..." She didn't get any further.

From across the room, someone was sounding the dinner gong very loudly, and calling for attention.

"Guests!" Lady Balmore addressed the room. "On behalf of the Earl and Countess Dunrannoch, I bid you welcome. We hope you enjoy the hospitality we're so pleased to share with you. Eat, drink and be merry."

A round of applause rippled through the room.

"There has been sorrow within these walls, but we must look to the future. I therefore suggest a toast to our new viscount—Lord Balmore."

Ursula felt herself blush to the roots as everyone around them turned to stare at herself and Rye, standing within the window alcove.

Arabella continued. "I know that Lady Fiona and her cousins will be eager for us to return to our dancing—" She smiled in the direction of her daughter. "But, I invite you to indulge in some festive merriment—a parlour game that was a favourite when I was a girl."

Her suggestion was met with an excited hum.

"I expect most of you are familiar with the rules. I shall select two guests to come and hide with me, somewhere in the castle. Your task, dear guests, shall be to find us within the hour and, when you do—singly, or in pairs—join us in that hiding place. When we gather ten, our tin of sardines shall be full and all who have completed their mission shall be rewarded with a prize!"

The applause, this time, was all the louder. Several of the footmen already had their eye on which of the maids they'd like to partner with, no doubt; skulking about the house in the dark would be reward in itself!

Ursula breathed a sigh of relief. Once the party dispersed through the house, she'd slip away. No one would even notice.

Arabella, however, hadn't finished.

"Without further ado, I invite Lord Balmore and Miss Abernathy to join me in seeking out a hiding place to baffle you all."

Holding out her hands like the good Moses, Lady Balmore parted the sea of guests, creating a path across the room directly from the window alcove to where she stood beside the gong.

"Hear, hear!" shouted someone.

"Show us how it's done Lord Balmore." Ursula was sure she recognized the first footman's voice.

With his usual beaming smile, Rye offered her his arm.

There was no escape!

"Excellent!" declared Lady Balmore. "Now, we need ten minutes head start. No one should come looking for us until we're well away."

Whisking them both before her, Arabella ushered them into the hallway.

"Now, my dears, as quickly as you can, follow me. I know just the place!"

CHAPTER NINETEEN

Mid-evening, 20th December

"DOWN THERE?" Rye squinted through the darkness beyond the door.

"Yes, go carefully on the steps. They're rather old and worn. Centuries of castle feet scraping up and down—although more down than up, of course, this being the dungeon." Arabella gave a tinkling laugh.

"It is a good hiding place, I s'pose." He gave Ursula's hand a tug. She'd gone mighty quiet and didn't seem at all keen on the game. It was the shock of the proposal, he guessed—and then the awkwardness of the whole room suddenly turning to look at them.

He knew ladies liked to take their time in deciding to become engaged and, despite his best intentions, he'd tumbled everything out like a man spilling his guts after one too many beers. Not the suavest of proposals, he had to admit—reminding her that she might have a bun in the oven.

Goddam, Rye. You could've done better!

But it couldn't be helped. He'd simply have to make it up to her.

If his grandmother could round up the pastor, they'd have a real Christmas wedding, with the bells ringing out for their happiness, as well as the day of Jesus' birth. Wouldn't that be something.

Arabella handed him a stump of candle and struck a match, taking an oil lamp for herself. "No one comes down here much, with it being so damp. No fireplaces for heating, just an old brazier the gaoler used to light." Arabella held up her lamp, leading them downward. "Best of all, there's a secret hiding place—one hardly anyone knows about. Brodie was excavating down here a few years ago and found what he thought was an old well, but the passageway leads to a hidden chamber. It's where they must have stashed the prisoners they really never wanted to lay eyes upon again. There were some remains…" Arabella lingered over the word, "But we had those removed, of course."

Rye felt Ursula shiver. Her eyes looked huge and her face so pale.

Was she afraid of the dark? He wasn't usually himself, but this place was darned spooky—and thinking about the poor wretches who'd been incarcerated made it worse.

"Chop, chop!" Arabella looked back at them. "We're almost there."

Reaching the bottom, she guided them through a narrow passageway, past several anterooms, until her illumination revealed a solid granite wall.

They could go no further, and he saw no sign of a well.

"Under our feet," Arabella lowered the lamp. "You see?" She kicked at the straw rushes that had been scattered over the earthen floor.

Bending, Rye made out the edges of something round and a good three feet in diameter.

"It's a lid of sorts," Arabella explained. "If we lift it, you'll see a rope ladder. Brodie attached it, to make it easier to get up and down. There's a drop of about ten feet and then you're in the chamber."

"They sure didn't do things by halves, did they." Working his fingers around the rim of the wooden cover, he prised it upward. Below, the darkness was palpable.

"You're sure about this Aunt Arabella?" Rye grimaced. "You don't think this might be going a little far?"

"Nonsense! Where's your spirit of fun?" Holding the lamp over the hole, she placed her hand on Rye's shoulder. "If you wouldn't mind going first; when you reach the bottom, you can keep the ladder steady for us to follow."

"As I'm the one wearing the kilt, that's probably the best idea." He laughed nervously then cleared his throat.

Passing the candle to Ursula, he lowered himself down. Sure enough, the rope seemed strong enough to hold him and, within a minute, he'd found the bottom.

"All safe and sound," he called up. "Come on, Ursula, I'm holding the ladder. There's nothing to be afraid of."

"I don't want to." Ursula's voice quivered.

Rye tilted back his head, peering up at the opening. He could see only the two women's faces, lit by a dull halo of lamplight.

Arabella laughed again. "Balderdash! We can't go back now. They'll already be looking for us."

"No!" Ursula announced more resolutely. She leaned over the hole. "Rye, you should climb back up. We shouldn't be down here. Something isn't right."

Arabella tutted. "It would have made things so much easier if you'd climbed down."

From above, Rye heard Ursula shriek.

Headfirst, she was tumbling through the air.

On instinct, Rye held out his arms and she fell straight into them, her weight knocking them both over.

"Dear God—Ursula!" Rye gasped. "Are you alright?" He

was sprawled on the ground beneath her, the air having been flattened from his lungs.

"Rye!" Ursula threw her arms around his neck, her voice terribly small. "Oh, Rye. She pushed me!"

"Ahoy down there." Arabella's voice drifted down. "Still alive?"

"I think so, but what the Hell, Arabella! You could've killed us!"

"Yes, that was the idea…" Lady Balmore clucked her tongue. "You just don't seem to take the hint. Quite tiresome, I must say."

Moving Ursula to one side, Rye got to his feet. The illumination had become fainter, as if Arabella had put the lamp to one side, but there was enough light to show the rope ladder disappearing upward. He jumped to grab hold but it was already out of reach.

"Hey, what are you doing? Arabella!" Rye was getting angry now. Whatever party game this was, it sure wasn't his idea of a good time.

"I'm leaving you entombed, you ridiculous man! You and that tart. Don't think I hadn't noticed. I warned Fiona not to bother with you. You weren't even supposed to turn up. The devil knows how Lavinia came up with the address for your father in the back of beyond!"

She made an unladylike spitting sound. "As if either of you could have stepped into my husband's shoes! He was worth ten of you—but that didn't make him good enough to take on the title, nor that pompous Lachlan. Mary's better off without him. I did her a favour, really. She'll see that in the end."

"Arabella? What are you talkin' about? It's true Ursula and I are in love, but she's no floozy. It might take some gettin' used to, but I hope you'll come round."

"Ha!" Arabella snorted. "The only thing I shall be 'coming round' to is Cameron taking the title of Viscount Balmore.

Once his position is secure, I'll help old Finlay on his way, and dear Cameron will be able to make me his countess."

Rye rubbed his ear and swallowed. He couldn't be hearing straight. Either that, or his aunt had taken a strange turn. He wasn't one for believing women prone to hysterics, but Arabella wasn't behaving like herself at all.

"I overheard them." Ursula tugged on Rye's sleeve. "It's true that there's something between her and Cameron. I think they were..." Ursula lowered her voice, "lovers!"

Rye nearly choked.

"Who do you think arranged for the bagpipes to play, making everyone think Camdyn was back, foretelling the deaths of the future lairds?" Arabella gave a cackle. "It wasn't easy persuading Buckie to go up onto the roof with the gramophone player. He made such a fuss about being afraid of heights, but I told him I'd strangle him in his bed unless he did as he was told. It was easier to get him to put the thistle under Brodie's saddle, and yours! As for Lachlan, I did that myself—a quick push down the staircase and the job was done."

Dear God! She was a murderess!

"Arabella! You can't just leave us here. Everyone will be looking." He scrambled to think of a way to bring her to her senses. "They know you were with us. Nobody will believe we got here by accident."

"I'll tell them I only led you as far as the upper corridor and have no idea where you've gone—that you begged me to let the two of you go off and canoodle on your own. I'm not the only one to have noticed you have a sweet spot for Miss Abernathy here. I'll come back when I can be sure you're dead and put the ladder through the open hole—with the rope shorn through, of course, so it looks as if it broke when you were climbing."

Far above, Arabella began nudging the lid back into place.

"You can't do this, Arabella. It's inhumane! It's criminal!"

Rye tried to keep the desperation from his voice, and failed miserably.

"It's fiendish!" added Ursula. "You're a bitch of the highest order!"

"I shall take that as a compliment. Now, I must go, my dears. Do enjoy the last few days together—or hours, possibly. The air isn't terribly fresh down here."

With that, the lid slid over completely and plunged them both into utter darkness.

CHAPTER TWENTY

Later that evening, 20th December

FROM THE FAR side of the room—which wasn't far enough, as far as Ursula was concerned—there was a scuffling sound.

A scuttling sort of scuffle, and a squeaking.

"Are those rats?"

"No, definitely not." Rye didn't sound convincing. "Mice maybe…or a hamster."

"A hamster?"

Rye had her on his lap, where she might sit without getting damp, and Ursula had her arms round his neck. She couldn't see him, but she could certainly feel him—warm and hard, and smelling a great deal better than anything else down here.

"Elsbeth and Blair keep them as pets. They might have escaped and come down here on an adventure."

"Of course. Why didn't I think of that?" she murmured, with more humour than she thought possible, given their present predicament.

"You probably would have, given time." Rye nuzzled her ear and poked his tongue into the whorl.

Ursula jumped and gave the back of his neck a pinch. "Stop that!"

"Don't you like it?" He chuckled.

"No. There are enough things down here that might be slimy without you sticking one in my ear."

"You know, it could be worse." Rye moved his right hand to cup the side of her bosom.

She shifted in his lap, but didn't slap the hand away. "You really think so?"

"There could be water rising around us." Rye gave the handful a light squeeze. "And there could be alligators in the water." With his other hand, he found the hem of her skirt and appropriated an ankle. "And piranhas swimming between the alligators."

"There aren't any piranhas in Perthshire. No alligators either." Ursula bent her knee and Rye scooted his left hand higher.

"All right. There could be spikes descending from the ceiling, gradually skewering us." Reaching her thigh, he fumbled for the top of her stocking.

"Skewering? I swear you have a one-track mind, Lord Balmore." She turned her head, searching out his lips. When she found them, he pulled her tight against his chest and kissed her deeply.

Everything had turned out horribly.

Arabella was a mad woman.

And they were probably going to die.

But they were together.

With her eyes closed, Ursula could nearly forget where they were. Forget that it was damp and cold, with water dripping down the walls, and vermin waiting for them to become too weak to fight off a carnivorous assault.

Rye's kisses were almost that good.

Almost.

They'd already tried shouting, and climbing up the walls. Neither had worked. No one had come.

"Are you ready to say 'yes'?" Rye brought her hands into her lap and held them with his own. She felt him draw out something from his pocket—cold metal brushing her fingers; his mother's ring.

Ursula sucked her lip.

She still hadn't quite forgiven him, but he'd told Arabella he loved her. That they loved each other, actually.

He'd said it without a moment's thought, as if it were the most natural thing in the world.

That must mean he believed it.

He'd defended her honour as well—telling that madwoman that she wasn't a floozy.

"You don't just want to marry me because I might already be having your baby?" It felt strange to ask when she wouldn't be able to see the expression on his face. How would she know if his answer was truthful? Would she be able to tell from his voice alone?

"Don't you know yet?" His hand came to her cheek. "I don't want to marry you because of what we did, or because you might have conceived. I want to marry you because I can't imagine you not being here. Now I've found you, I don't want you to go away. I want you here with me, Ursula, always."

She smiled. "If I'm going to die, I suppose I might as well die engaged."

She couldn't see it, but she knew that Rye was smiling.

He slid the ring right onto her finger. "That's the spirit."

WHEN THE WOODEN lid slid back and lantern light filled the opening, it seemed so bright that Rye could hardly bear to look.

Cameron called both their names.

"By all that's holy, I'm glad to see you." Shielding his eyes, Rye waved his hand.

"She's gone off her rocker!" Cameron's voice was shaking. "I'd no idea, I swear, but she told me everything—including that she'd shut you in here."

Rye reached down to pull Ursula to her feet. "Get that rope ladder down here, buddy. It's been a helluva party, but I'm ready to call it a night. Get us out of here, and you can tell us everything."

"To think that, for a while, I thought I might be in love with her." Cameron could barely bring himself to look Rye, or Ursula, in the face. "I've been trying to break it off for months."

"We all make mistakes." Climbing out behind Ursula, Rye resisted the temptation to slap Cameron's injured shoulder. "But didn't the others get curious about where we'd gone?"

"Your grandfather was convinced that Arabella's story was true—that you two had gone off to… you know." Cameron gave an apologetic shrug, then winced, clutching his shoulder. "He said you and he had had a long talk earlier in the day and you'd told him you were going to ask Miss Abernathy to marry you. It all added up. It was only when we were sending the last guests to bed that Arabella pounced on me. She was so excited, telling me how she'd planned everything, starting with killing Brodie." He shuddered and passed his hand over his face.

Rye had to admit, Cameron looked as sick about it as Rye felt. But had only a few hours passed? It felt as if they'd been in that hole for days.

"Where is she now?" Rye had to know.

"I left her sobbing in her room. I made it clear that anything between us was over. She's in a bad way." Cameron gave Rye a pleading look. "I'm not sure what she'll do next— whether she'll hurt herself."

Rye turned to Ursula. "We'll get you something warm to drink and I'll light the fire in your room, then I'll go with Cameron. It's too much for him to deal with on his own. We may have to lock Arabella in, until we work out how to handle this."

"There's no time for that." Ursula squeezed Rye's hand. "We need to see Arabella first. She's a danger to more than herself. We can't leave her on the loose."

"That's my little bear." Rye dropped a kiss on Ursula's forehead.

"Follow me," said Ursula. "It's quickest to take the servants' stairs."

AS THEY TURNED onto the corridor in which Arabella's bedchamber was sited, they were in time to see her emerging from the room.

"You!" She screeched at Cameron. "Betrayer! After all I did for you."

"Arabella, calm down. We can talk this through." Cameron inched along the passageway.

"There's nothing to talk about, you weasel! I don't know what I ever saw in you."

"Come back! Arabella!" Cameron called out, but it was too late.

Lifting her skirts, Lady Balmore ran in the opposite direction.

"She's heading for the battlements!" Cameron looked as if he was about to pass out. He staggered and half-fell but urged Rye on. "Go after her, please. Don't let her do anything stupid."

Round and round they climbed, Rye ahead and Ursula doing her best to keep up, taking the spiral steps of stone, past each floor until they reached the door leading onto the roof.

Rye gasped as he emerged into the night air. A hard frost was forming, coating every surface in a sheen of ice.

And it was so quiet. Quieter than the dungeon had been.

He couldn't see Arabella at first—only the stars and the sky.

The sky was huge, and the stars brighter than he'd ever seen them, up here, high above the moor.

Ursula grabbed the back of his shirt. "Where is she?" She was panting hard, having run all the way.

"Look, there." He saw her now, the wind whisking her long hair, tumbling from its pins. And she'd climbed up onto the ramparts.

"Arabella!" Ursula called. "Come down from there."

Lady Balmore turned, and there was a madness in her eyes. "Come here then, if you want to help me." She stretched out her arm, beckoning.

"No, Ursula!" But Rye wasn't quick enough. Ursula had darted past him, running to Lady Balmore.

"Wait!" Ursula's voice was whipped by the breeze. She'd almost reached her.

"No time to wait," answered Lady Balmore. Her fingers touched Ursula's and pulled her up beside her. "You'll go with me, then. I won't be alone." With that, Lady Balmore leant forward.

There was a flutter of fabric and a shriek.

"Ursula!" Rye grabbed her waist and yanked her back.

He'd nearly lost her.

So very nearly.

From far below came a hollow thud.

EPILOGUE

Christmas Day

"Mistletoe? In your bridal crown?" Mary pursed her lips, looking over Ursula's ensemble one last time—even though they were standing just inside the door of the castle chapel and it was really too late to change anything. "Are you quite sure?"

Miss Abernathy might have owned up to being closely related to the Arrington viscountcy but Mary was still a little suspicious. In her eyes, decent women didn't go galavanting about the Highlands pretending to be something they weren't.

"She looks lovely!" declared Lady Dunrannoch. "I only worry that you're warm enough, Ursula dear. Even with your thickest underthings, this place is as cold as the tomb."

The countess was far more willing to reconcile herself to Ursula's new status. Clearly, young Rye was smitten—and the girl was nothing if not resourceful. She'd hold her own amongst the Dalreaghs, Lady Dunrannoch was certain.

Iona's wedding dress, which had been handed down from the old dowager herself, had only needed the tiniest of alterations. The lace, freshly whitened with lemon juice, was studded with tiny pearls across the bodice and down each sleeve, and the wide, square-neck of the gown was most becoming. With silver slippers and a long veil of silk tulle, Ursula's costume was complete.

With all that had happened, it was only fitting for the wedding to be a quiet affair, but Rye was determined that their joy would push tragedy aside.

They were sharing that joy with the people who really mattered. Both Daphne and Eustace had made the journey, thanks to Campbell riding out to send telegrams, and all the family were gathered.

As Earl Dunrannoch walked Ursula down the aisle to meet her groom, Rye looked round and gave her that lopsided Dalreagh smile. The one that told her she was the person he most wanted to see in the whole wide world, and the one he wanted to kiss. The one he wanted to spend his life with—no matter what life ended up throwing at them.

What had Miss Abernathy's *Lady's Guide* said? She'd been looking for advice on marriage and husbands, and the book had a lot to say on the subject—some of it bizarre, but most of it rather good. Or, at least, it seemed so.

There had been something about not finding your happiness by running away, and that, when you found the right person, you'd know it was time to stop running all together. That you could stand still, instead, and know you were right where you were supposed to be.

Ursula had that feeling.

She didn't need to run away from Rye.

He wasn't marrying her because that was what his family were insisting upon.

He wasn't marrying her from any sense of duty.

And he wasn't marrying her for her inheritance. She knew this for certain because she still hadn't told him, although she'd had to come clean to the pastor about her real name, and to Rye too, for the sake of legalities. It had been time to own up to not being Miss Abernathy and, strangely enough, Rye hadn't acted in the least surprised, nor appeared to care.

He was making her his because he wanted her in his arms and in his heart, and he wanted to face every bit of what came next together.

When he looked deep into her eyes, she saw that he looked serious, and just a little nervous.

"You ready to take the leap, little bear?"

"I am—if you're jumping with me."

There was the smile again. "We're gonna jump right in together." He pressed his lips to her ear. "You and me. Every day, over and over."

And Ursula smiled right back.

Meanwhile, from the battlements, the ghost of Camdyn Dalreagh looked down. He'd put away his bagpipes for the time being, having no intention of playing them any time soon. Instead, he'd tucked McTavish under his arm.

Together, they'd watch over Castle Dunrannoch and the newlyweds.

McTavish would surely leave an occasional offering on the crisp quilt of Lord and Lady Balmore's bedchamber, but it would always be given with love.

BONUS MATERIAL

If you enjoyed 'The Lady's Guide to Mistletoe and Mayhem', you'll adore Emmanuelle de Maupassant's 1920s romantic comedy series set in the Highlands of Scotland.

Intrigue, seduction and a dash of wicked humour, for fans of Rhys Bowen, Stella Gibbons and Nancy Mitford.

Highland Pursuits
It's 1928 and Bright Young Things are taking London by storm, but Ophelia's parents have her life all mapped out:

marriage to a cod-faced aristocrat and a life of dull respectability.

Refusing to play along, Ophelia is banished to her ancestral home in the Highlands of Scotland. There, she'll be so bored, she'll come to her senses... won't she?

Meeting her eccentric relatives, Ophelia isn't so sure, and there's utter mayhem as guests arrive for her grandmother's birthday celebrations.

Amidst the faded splendour of Castle Kintochlochie, everyone is having a ball, until tragedy strikes on a moorland shoot.

Nothing is quite as it seems!

Highland Christmas
As Christmas approaches, and the snow falls deep, could Lady Ophelia's life be in danger?

Someone, or something, is determined to derail Ophelia's love affair with Hamish. A malevolent force stalks the ancient corridors of Castle Kintochlochie, in its remote Highland glen. Is the castle really haunted?

ABOUT EMMANUELLE DE MAUPASSANT

Emmanuelle lives with her husband (maker of tea and fruit cake) and has a penchant for hairy pudding terriers (connoisseurs of squeaky toys and bacon treats). She most especially loves the Scottish Highlands.

Want to read more in this series, as new titles are released?
'The Lady's Guide to Escaping Cannibals'
'The Lady's Guide to a Highlander's Heart'
'The Lady's Guide to a Sultan's Harem'
'The Lady's Guide to Scandal'
'The Lady's Guide to Deception and Desire'

Sign up to Emmanuelle's newsletter and hear all the latest, straight to your inbox
Just visit her website to join -
www.emmanuelledemaupassant.com

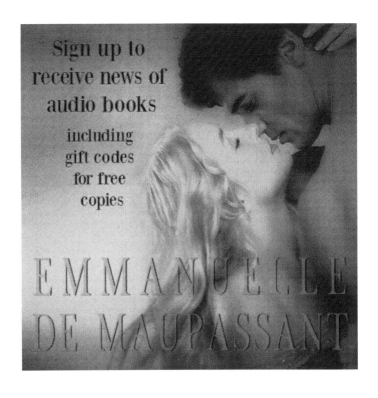

Love Audio Books?
Visit Emmanuelle's website to become part of her Audio Book Club.
Hear about her new releases in audio - including gift codes for free audio books.

www.emmanuelledemaupassant.com

Printed in Great Britain
by Amazon

59650017R00097